NO WAY OUT

ADAM CROFT

**BLACK CANNON
PUBLISHING**

First published in Great Britain in 2024.

This edition published in 2024 by Black Cannon Publishing.

ISBN: 978-1-912599-79-0

A CIP catalogue record for this book is available from the British Library.

Printed and bound in Great Britain by Clays Ltd, Elcograf S.p.A.

- In Her Image
- Tell Me I'm Wrong
- The Perfect Lie
- Closer To You

KEMPSTON HARDWICK MYSTERIES

1. Exit Stage Left
2. The Westerlea House Mystery
3. Death Under the Sun
4. The Thirteenth Room
5. The Wrong Man

All titles are available to order from all good book shops.

Signed and personalised editions available at adamcroft.net.

Foreign language editions of some titles are available in French, German, Italian, Portuguese, Dutch and Korean. These are available online and in book shops in their native countries.

EBOOK-ONLY SHORT STORIES

- Gone
- The Harder They Fall
- Love You To Death
- The Defender
- Thick as Thieves
- Silent Echoes

To find out more, visit adamcroft.net.

EXCLUSIVE MEMBERSHIP BENEFITS

Are you an avid reader of my books? If so, you can gain access to exclusive members-only books, content and more.

By subscribing to VIP Premium, you'll get a whole host of benefits and additional perks — and supporting me and my work directly.

Here are just a few of the benefits you can enjoy:

- **Up to 30% off** all online shop orders from adamcroft.net
- **Early access to new books** — up to *2 weeks* before release
- A **free ebook** of your choice
- **Free short stories**, not available anywhere else
- Have a **character named after you** in future books
- Access to **exclusive** videos and behind-the-scenes content
- A **personalised video message** from me
- Unlimited **free UK postage** (and reduced international shipping)

- **Your name in the Acknowledgements** of every new book
- Access to **exclusive** blog posts

To find out more, or to join today, head to **adamcroft. net/membership.**

HAVE YOU LISTENED TO THE RUTLAND AUDIOBOOKS?

The Rutland crime series is now available in audiobook format, narrated by Leicester-born **Andy Nyman** (Peaky Blinders, Unforgotten, Star Wars) and **Mathew Horne** (Gavin & Stacey, The Catherine Tate Show, Horne & Corden).

The series is available from all good audiobook retailers and libraries now, published by W.F. Howes on their QUEST and Clipper imprints.

W.F. Howes are one of the world's largest audiobook publishers and have been based in Leicestershire since their inception.

W . F . H O W E S LTD

QUEST

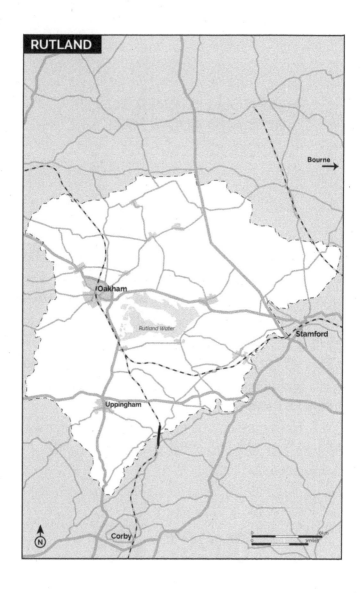

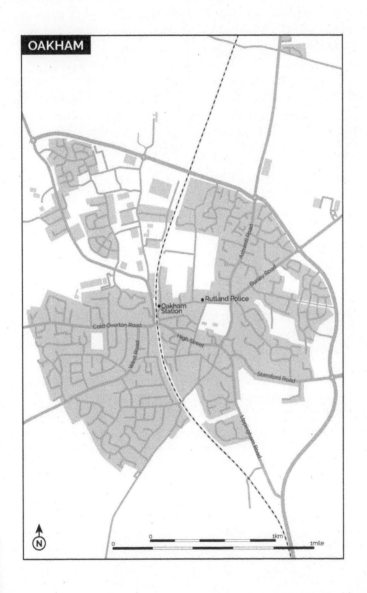

For Sarah, Amie, Fiona, James, Lucas and Ava.

1

Linda Harrington tutted to herself as she shook the rainwater from the discarded crisp packet and popped it in her plastic sack.

She wanted to believe the previous night's storm was to blame for much of the mess, but deep down she knew things were hardly perfect on any other Saturday.

Her weekly litter pick was something she enjoyed, although of course she wished she didn't have to do it. It was more that it gave her that familiar feeling of doing something for her community, and improving the area they all had to live in.

She groaned inwardly as she realised how full her rubbish sack was already. She knew she should have brought more. At this rate, her litter picker was going to need its hinges oiling.

The party at the Blackwood house had kept her – and the rest of Upper Hambleton – awake as much as the storm, although she was secretly thankful both had happened on the same evening. Had the revellers fancied a late-night wander around the peninsula, or ended up spilling out into the streets, she'd've had an awful lot more beer cans and bottles to pick up.

Both she and her next-door neighbour, Sheila, had phoned the police to report the nuisance party, but they were told there was nothing they could do. They were short-staffed, the road onto the peninsula was impassable due to fallen trees, and – in the words of the police call handler – 'they'll have had enough and finish before too long, I'm sure'. *Well I've already bloody well had enough*, Linda wanted to reply, but didn't.

She remembered a time when it seemed people had respect, and often wondered who or what was responsible for the continuous race to the bottom when it came to behaviour and standards. What concerned her most was that she'd probably taught most of their parents. She reckoned she could probably take a good guess at which ones, too.

Although she'd never admit it – or even recognise it – it was something that gave her life purpose. She, like many people (and all teachers) had spent her whole working life counting down to retirement. She and Richard had often talked about their plans, and had been so looking forward to travelling the world and enjoying a good twenty or thirty more years together without the worry of work. But three words had taken that away from them: subacute spongiform encephalopathy.

She could still hear those words in the consultant's voice the first time he'd said it. She knew the last word likely had something to do with the brain, but it wasn't until the consultant had fully explained it that she finally began to understand. It was more commonly known as Creutzfeldt-Jakob disease, and Richard's was already advanced by the time he'd been diagnosed.

It had been obvious something was wrong. Memory loss, mood changes, balance and coordination issues: they could all have been caused by a hundred and one different conditions. Some form of dementia was feared, but at least that could have given them a matter of years together. CJD, however, had taken Richard in just eleven weeks.

It had all been so unbelievably cruel. Richard had worked so hard every day of his life and had been rewarded with barely six months of retirement, four of which had been blighted by illness and more than two of them knowing he was staring a certain and imminent death in the face. At times it had seemed like something of a blessing that he hadn't been entirely with it. How aware had he been of what was going on? Did he even realise? Had he felt the same crushing panic and fear that she had?

Even now, five years on, it sometimes felt as though he'd walk through the door at any minute, as if returning from a lengthy holiday. There had never seemed to be any chance whatsoever of him dying before his time was up. He'd always been incredibly active. The man had represented his country in the Commonwealth Games, for crying out loud.

She knew she'd never truly be happy again. Not like she had been. But she was at least content, satisfied that she was doing the best she could with what she had. And community involvement gave her that same sense of satisfaction and reward it had always given her. It was what had driven her to become a teacher, and it was what now drove her to get out of bed at six o'clock each Saturday morning and walk the peninsula with her trusty 928mm Unger with magnetic tip and 360 degree rotating head.

She usually managed an hour or two, depending on the weather, before popping the bags in the back of her car and taking them off to the Cottesmore Household Waste Recycling Centre – the only place she frequented more often than the Co-Op.

Despite the previous night's storm, it was shaping up to be a beautiful day. The mugginess of the past few days had lifted, and it already felt easier to breathe. A sleepless night was a small price to pay for having cleared the oppressive humidity that had been lingering for what felt like an age.

Linda followed the footpath down towards the next field, stopping occasionally to pick up more pieces of litter that had likely escaped from an upended wheelie bin god knows how many hundreds of yards away. Then there were the countless branches, twigs and sticks that the trees had shed in last night's wind. She cleared those from the path as best she could, so that no-one would trip over or end up with half a tree mangled in their bike chain, but if she'd picked them all up she'd have no room for litter.

As she stepped through into the field, she let out an involuntary groan at the sight of the pile of clothes that had been dumped unceremoniously in the long grass. What on earth possessed people to drive all the way out here to dump their rubbish when they could have easily taken it to the tip? She realised there was no point in even asking herself that question, because she knew there was no answer.

She reached into her pocket for her mobile phone, ready to call the environmental department at the council, but something stopped her. It was a strange sense of foreboding at the sight of something seemingly innocuous. It was a feeling she'd last had when Richard's consultant had walked into the waiting room at the hospital, briefly flashing them a friendly but ultimately empty smile. This time, though, it was the second glance at the pile of clothes.

Although the clothes themselves didn't give Linda any cause for alarm, the grey leg sticking out from under them did.

2

Caroline sunk her teeth into her bacon sandwich, the salt and fat washing over her tastebuds in a way that could never quite be matched by any other food.

'Oh for bloody hell's sake!' Mark shouted, getting to his feet and marching over to the kitchen window. 'You have got to be kidding me!'

'What is it?' Caroline asked, crumbs tumbling from her mouth.

'The bloody parasol's gone right through our shed window! I thought it was clamped to the table?'

'It was.'

'Well it's not anymore. It's sticking out of the shed like a cocktail umbrella. Christ, I suppose everything in there's going to be soaking wet now, isn't it?'

'It's only outdoor stuff,' Caroline replied, looking back down at the news article she'd been reading on her phone.

'Cushions for the garden chairs, the kids' bikes. Nothing that won't dry out again.'

Mark shoved his hands in his pockets. 'Not really the point, is it?'

'I'll have a word with Mother Nature for you. See if we can get her to apologise.'

'There's no need to be like that,' Mark replied, looking like a scolded child.

'Well what do you want anyone to do about it? It's a storm. Things get damaged. If you leave them in the middle of the garden, anyway.'

'What's that meant to mean?'

Caroline sighed. 'I did say it might be worth putting the parasol in the shed before the storm came in.'

'It was meant to be clamped securely to the table,' Mark replied through gritted teeth. 'Anyway, it *is* in the shed now.'

'There you go then. Nothing to complain about.'

'I'll remind you of that when you're picking shards of glass out of your backside next time you want to sit on those cushions.'

Caroline let out a groan. 'Oh for Christ's sake, we'll get some new cushions then. I'm sure they'll do them in B&Q with the replacement shed windows.'

'Which I suppose I'm going to have to fit,' Mark huffed.

'I'm more than happy to help. Even though it wouldn't have happened if–'

'Yeah, don't.'

Caroline raised her hands in mock surrender, watching as Mark's attention was taken, and his frustration fuelled, by the clock on the oven.

'And now I've got to spend the next half an hour trying to remember how to set this thing, I suppose. Bloody power cuts. Why can't these electronic clocks set themselves in this day and age? I mean, it can switch itself on and cook an entire roast dinner for us while we're not even in the house, but if you turn the wrong plug off you've got to sit here jabbing it with a bloody paperclip all morning.'

'I'll set the clocks,' Caroline said. 'It's fine. You've got a watch. And a phone.'

'A phone with no internet connection because the router decided to reset itself after the power cut.'

'You don't need the internet to see the time.'

'It's not the point,' Mark replied, with a tone of voice that sounded like a child who'd just been told he had to visit his least favourite aunt.

Caroline dug her thumbnails into the sides of her forefingers as she tried to push down her own frustration. 'Yes, well it's how it is, so we're just going to have to deal with it, alright?'

Mark looked at her quizzically. 'What's got into you?' he asked.

Caroline let out an involuntary laugh. 'Excuse me? What's got into me? I've had to sit here all morning listening to you moaning on and on about things that I – no, no-one – can do a single thing about. Things that could have been avoided if you'd just… Look, forget it. It doesn't matter. None of it matters. Not today.'

'Why did you say it like that?' Mark asked.

Caroline looked back down at her phone. 'It doesn't matter.'

'It was March when we got married,' her husband said, with all the confidence of someone who'd been asked how many post boxes there were in the UK.

Caroline sighed for what felt like the umpteenth time that morning. 'It's not *our* anniversary, no.'

'Then what… Oh.'

'Yes,' Caroline replied. 'Oh.'

Mark walked over to her and put a hand on her shoulder. 'I'm sorry, Caz. I didn't realise. I mean, obviously I knew. I just…'

'It's fine.'

For the first few years, the anniversary of her brother Stuart's death had been a day of huge significance for Caroline and her family. August the seventeenth had loomed ominously on the calendar for weeks before, staring at them like an immovable force that they had no choice but to face head on. But with each year that passed, that had become a little easier.

In recent years, it was now more often a case of noticing on the day itself, or at most a couple of days before. That wasn't to say it had become less significant, because it hadn't. Caroline still hadn't experienced a single seventeenth of August that wasn't shrouded in a black cloud, but now she at least had the comfort of knowing she could and would get through it, as she had so many times before.

Getting through it wasn't the same as getting over it, of course. No-one ever quite got over the death of a loved one, particularly in tragic circumstances, but for Caroline there was a lot more to get over.

Caroline's phone began to ring, dissolving – and then quickly reintroducing – the awkward atmosphere in the room.

She looked down at the screen, then up at Mark.

'Work?' he asked, a look of slight resignation on his face.

Caroline nodded. 'Work.'

3

'I think this is as far as we get,' Dexter said, pulling his car gently up onto the grass verge and coming to a halt. He switched the engine off. 'I still can't believe the amount of damage that storm's caused here. It didn't even touch Leicester.'

'Lucky you,' Caroline replied, unbuckling her seatbelt. 'Our shed got speared like a kebab.'

'Woah. By what?'

'An umbrella. Long story.'

They got out of the car and greeted the uniformed officer who was standing by a fallen tree, which had completely blocked both sides of the road. Police tape covered its length.

'At least Mother Nature had the decency to provide us with an outer cordon,' Dexter quipped. 'Will save us a fortune on tape, too.'

'Seemed as good a place as any,' the officer replied, smiling. 'It's quite a walk to the inner cordon, mind. Know where you're going?'

'Nope.'

'Quickest way is to carry on straight down here and into the village, past the pub, and opposite the post box you'll see a footpath off to your left. Head down there, and you can't miss it.'

'Got it,' Dexter replied. 'Is it far?'

'About a mile. Twenty minutes or so to walk it.'

'You've got to be joking,' Caroline said, her shoulders slumping.

'Not much we can do,' the officer replied, gesturing to the fallen tree. 'Unless you want to try driving over this.'

'Not a chance,' Dexter said, before Caroline could say a word. 'That thing struggles with speed bumps.'

'You want to try slowing down for them, then,' Caroline replied.

Dexter grinned. 'And where's the fun in that?'

The pair set off on foot, clambering over the fallen tree and continuing to make their way along the main road, Rutland Water opening up on both sides of them.

'Bit like an Agatha Christie, this one, innit?' Dexter said.

Caroline knew exactly what he meant. There was a particularly eerie atmosphere that she couldn't quite put her finger on, almost as if the calm had come after the storm. Not only that, but it was starting to look as if they might have their very own form of locked-room mystery.

With the storm damage and fallen trees blocking the Oakham Road, there was no other way off the peninsula unless you had a boat or were a particularly brave swimmer. And Caroline was willing to bet her bottom dollar that no-one would be stupid enough to have attempted to sail or swim across Rutland Water in the middle of the night with a storm raging.

Rutland Water's distinctive horseshoe shape was entirely down to Upper Hambleton being where it was – on high ground, overlooking what would previously have been the valleys below with the bustling village of Nether Hambleton, but which were now the depths of one of Europe's biggest manmade lakes.

It had long fascinated Caroline that the main road along the peninsula – Oakham Road – became Ketton Road once you got to Upper Hambleton itself. The Ketton Road continued along the peninsula, ending abruptly at the shore of Rutland Water, Normanton Church visible in the distance on the far shore. Beside the church on the other side of the water, the road continued again, on towards Ketton, as if nothing had ever happened.

The atmosphere grew even more tense as Caroline and Dexter rounded the final corner and took in the scene in front of them, inside what would now become the inner cordon. A uniformed officer at the scene introduced herself as PC Amanda Robinson. She gave them a brief rundown of the situation so far.

'Looks like a young woman, somewhere roughly between eighteen and twenty-one years of age. She was found by a woman who was out litter picking. She does that every Saturday morning, apparently. She says she didn't disturb the body or make contact with it. It's a bit out in the open here, and we didn't have the scene secured. Plus there's been a bit of activity around the village this morning. Word's already got round, of course. There was a party in one of the local houses last night. Teenagers. About her age,' the officer said, nodding her head towards the young woman's lifeless body. 'One of the girls apparently disappeared at some point during the party, but nobody quite knows when. I think there'd been a fair bit of drink floating around. As well as other things, I dare say. The description they gave of their friend does match the IP. Even the way they described her clothes.'

'Where's the house?' Caroline asked.

'Literally just behind these trees here,' PC Robinson replied. 'You walked past it on the way in. I can take you there once I've got cover here.'

'Excellent, thanks. What's the identity of the IP?'

'If it's the girl we think it is, her name's Emily Ashcroft. Twenty-one years of age. Her friends said she had long blonde hair, and was wearing a white crop top and a short denim skirt. It matches what we've got here. The party was pretty lively, by all accounts. We actually received a couple of reports about it overnight, but didn't have anyone able to attend.'

'No strong swimmers on the night shift?' Caroline asked.

'Apparently not. According to the other kids at the party, it pretty much died off when there was a power cut and the music cut out.'

Caroline smiled. 'How'd you get here?' she asked.

'From the roadblock, you mean? I ran.'

'Crikey. Alright for you,' Caroline replied. 'I could barely walk it.'

PC Robinson smiled. 'I play for Oakham United Women. When shifts allow, I mean.'

'So what's that, twice a season?'

Her smile became a smirk. 'Something like that. Oh, I forgot to mention. Some locals were offering to move the fallen tree out of the way. I didn't really know if it was best to preserve everything just in case, or if you'd want it moved to help access but I thought I'd play it safe. I figured you'd order it moved if you needed it moved.'

Caroline agreed. 'Despite what my legs and lungs are telling me, you did the right thing.' She thought back to Dexter's comments and her musings about the fallen tree providing them with a limited list of suspects. 'When did the tree come down?' she asked.

'First report came in just before ten last night,' PC Robinson replied. 'No idea how long it'd been down by then, though. I don't imagine too many people were driving around aimlessly at that point. Half the roads had flooded, anyway.'

'Alright. Dex, can you authorise the tree to be cleared. We'll need to get ambo and forensics units in here, and there's no way they'll want to walk it. Get it replaced with a manned roadblock, though. No-one allowed to exit the peninsula, and entry only with SIO authorisation. Got it?'

'Got it. Well, except one thing,' Dexter replied.

Caroline gave a sympathetic sigh as a smile broke across her face. 'Yes, Dex,' she said. 'That's you.'

4

Once the forensics team had erected their tent over the area of Emily Ashcroft's body, Caroline and Dexter made it their priority to head to the house where last night's party had been held.

As they reached the impressive property, they were slightly taken aback by the incongruous sight of two young men sitting on the front steps, vaping, the front door to the house open behind them. In any other situation, Caroline's instinct would have been that she was dealing with a group of squatters.

'Morning, lads. How're your heads?' Dexter asked.

'Been better,' one of them replied. 'You police?'

'Is it really that obvious?'

The young man gave a small grin. 'Is a bit.'

'Is it your house?' Dexter asked.

'Nah. His mum and dad's,' he replied, elbowing his friend in the side.

'Yeah, and they're gonna kill me when they get back.' He froze for a moment, before backpedaling. 'I mean… Shit. Bad choice of words.'

'What're your names, lads?' Caroline asked.

'Liam Carter,' the first boy replied.

'Dan Blackwood,' the other said. 'Daniel.'

'Where are your folks, Dan?'

'They went away for the weekend. Norfolk or something. They're back tomorrow. Am I gonna have to ring them?'

Caroline and Dexter exchanged a glance.

'I think we might have to let them know what's happened,' Dexter said. 'By any luck they might have calmed down by tomorrow.'

'It's her then?' Dan replied, a resigned look on his face.

'We still need to complete an official identification. But it's looking likely. We're going to have to ask you some questions too,' Caroline said.

'We've already told the other officer everything we know,' Dan said, looking worried. 'Do we have to go through it all again?'

'It's important we get a clear picture,' Dexter said. 'Can we come in?'

'Yeah, course,' Dan said, standing up and leading them inside. The house was a mess, with empty bottles and cans scattered everywhere, and the lingering smell of smoke and alcohol hung in the air.

'How many people were here?' Caroline asked as they

walked into the living room, where a few other groggy-looking young adults were sprawled on the sofas.

'About twenty, maybe more,' Dan said. 'It was supposed to be a small thing, but then more people showed up. You know how it is.'

'We'll need a list of everyone who was here,' Dexter said. 'Names, contact details, anything you've got.'

'Yeah, okay,' Dan said, looking dazed. 'I'll try to get that for you.'

'Most of them are still around, sleeping upstairs. There's a few in the cinema room out the back, too. No-one could get home 'cos of the storm.'

'We'll need to talk to everyone who was here,' Caroline said. 'Can you tell us who Emily's closest friends were? We'll need to start with them.'

Liam nodded. 'Her best mate was Lucy. Last I heard, she was in the kitchen.'

'Alright,' Caroline replied. 'We'll start there.'

Liam led them down the hall to the kitchen, where they found Lucy sitting at the table, staring blankly at a cup of tea. Her eyes were red from crying, and she looked up as they entered.

'Lucy?' Caroline asked gently.

Lucy nodded. 'Yes.'

'I'm Detective Inspector Caroline Hills, and this is Detective Sergeant Dexter Antoine. We're very sorry for your loss, Lucy. We know this is difficult, but we need to ask you some questions about Emily and the party last night.'

Lucy took a deep breath, trying to steady herself. 'Okay. I'll do my best.'

'How did you know Emily? Dan says you were good friends.'

'Yeah,' Lucy replied, tears welling in her eyes. 'We'd been best friends since we were kids. We lived round the corner from each other growing up. Went to the same schools, same uni. Even managed to blag rooms in the same halls.'

Dexter gave a sympathetic smile. 'It sounds like you went back a long way.'

'We did. I... My parents died just before my third birthday. They were driving back from a gala dinner when their car was taken out by a lorry driver who'd fallen asleep at the wheel.'

'I'm sorry to hear that,' Dexter replied.

Lucy gave a slight shrug. 'It's a long time ago. I never really knew them. My mum's sister and her husband adopted me. I've always called them Mum and Dad. We met Emily shortly after that. She lived round the corner and we used to see her at the same park. Then we ended up in the same pre-school. My parents left quite a lot of money, and Mum and Dad used that later on to send me to private school. Emily's parents were always going to do the same too, so circumstances brought us together and kept us together too.'

Dexter smiled. 'And you went to the same university, you said?'

'Yeah, Leicester. Oh god… I've just realised. I'll need to tell Sophie.'

'Who's Sophie?' Dexter asked.

'A friend from uni. Well, she's from Oakham, but we only met at uni. She's going to be heartbroken.'

Dexter sensitively took Sophie's details from Lucy, making a note that she might be someone who could provide them with some information. 'It's nice to see people staying fairly local for university,' he said. 'Makes a change from kids wanting to get as far away from Rutland as possible.'

'I think we wanted enough independence and adventure without going too far from home. I don't think her parents were too happy.'

'Why's that?'

'I think they'd expected her to go to Oxford or Cambridge, especially considering all the money they'd spent on sending her to private school. Her dad's a bit like that. He says she wasted it on a "Mickey Mouse subject at a Mickey Mouse university".'

'Charming,' Dexter replied, filing this away mentally. Perpetually disappointed parents were always interesting cases. 'You say you went to the same school and uni, though. What did your parents make of it?'

Lucy blinked and looked away.

'Shit. Sorry,' Dexter said, immediately realising his mistake. 'I mean your… you know.'

'Aunt and uncle. Mum and Dad.'

'Yeah.'

'They were really supportive. They just wanted me to be happy. They're not private school kind of people. If it'd been up to them they would've put the money away to help me on the housing ladder or something, but my parents had it in their wills that it was for my education, so… Yeah. Funny how people can still completely steer your life even though they're six feet underground.'

Dexter gave a slight smile. 'I'm sure they just wanted the best for you. Can you tell us about how Emily was last night?' he asked. 'Did she seem upset or worried about anything?'

Lucy nodded slowly. 'She did. She kept checking her phone, like she was waiting for someone. She wouldn't tell me what was going on, though. She just said she had to meet someone.'

'Do you know who?'

Lucy shook her head. 'No, she didn't say.'

'What time did anybody last see her?'

'About midnight, we think. Everyone saw her at some point, but we weren't all looking at the clock.'

'Do you know if anyone else left the party? Even for a short while,' Dexter asked.

'I don't think so. Not that I noticed, anyway.'

Whilst Dexter continued talking to Lucy, Caroline stepped outside and into the large garden at the back of the house.

Before long, Dan Blackwood sidled up beside her.

'Look, this is probably nothing,' Dan said, 'but Liam and Lucy had a fight last night.'

Caroline cocked her head. 'A fight?'

'Yeah. Outside. I didn't see how it started – I just saw Liam shoving Lucy over – but I think it was about Emily.'

'What makes you think it was about her?' Caroline asked.

Dan let out a harrumph. 'I'm guessing Liam didn't tell you Emily was his girlfriend.'

Caroline tried not to let the surprise show on her face. 'He didn't, as it happens. Were they serious?'

Dan shrugged. 'A year or so, on and off. Maybe more.'

'Okay. So back to the fight last night. How much did you witness?'

'Not much. To be fair, it's only because there was a gap between songs and I was by the window, but I heard Lucy shouting at him. Couldn't work out what it was all about, but by the time I'd worked out what it was and was looking at them, they were right in each other's faces. Then Liam just shoved her over and walked off.'

'Walked off where?'

'Back into the house.'

'Did you speak to him?'

'Didn't get a chance. A couple of his mates had seen it at the same time as me and they went over to take him off to another room and calm him down. You can't go doing stuff like that.'

'And what about Lucy? Where did she go?'

'She just stayed there for a few seconds. She'd sat up, but looked sort of stunned. I was gonna go out and help her, check she was alright, but by the time I'd got to the door she was back up and on her way in.'

'Okay. Did you speak to her?'

'Yeah, but not much. I just sort of said "are you okay" sort of thing, and she was like "yeah", and and saying he was a dick and stuff. She looked well upset. Lucy's a real nice girl. I think it just really shocked her.'

'And where did she go after that?' Caroline asked.

'She went off to the bathroom. Said she was going to dry herself off and take a few minutes to sort herself out. She was soaked, obviously, 'cause of the rain. And she had mud all up her from where she'd hit the ground.'

Caroline nodded. 'What time was the fight? Do you know?'

'I can't say for sure, but it was after midnight. Look, please don't tell anyone I told you this.'

Caroline thought about this for a few seconds. It was odd that Liam Carter hadn't mentioned he'd been in a relationship with Emily Ashcroft, who was lying dead just a couple of hundred metres away. And it was even more curious that he was seen assaulting her best friend on the same night she was killed.

She thanked Dan Blackwood for his time, and reconvened with Dexter once he'd finished speaking with Lucy, and updated him on what Dan had told her.

Dexter nodded slowly. 'Doesn't take long for the loyalty to crack, does it?'

5

Not long after they'd spoken to Liam Carter and Lucy Palmer, the road was clear again and Caroline and Dexter headed to the station for the first team briefing.

Dexter stood at the front of the room, with Caroline perched on the edge of a desk nearby. Detective Constables Aidan Chilcott and Sara Henshaw were sat at their desks, and Detective Sergeant Elijah Drummond was leaning against a wall, one hand holding a mug of coffee, the other shoved in his trouser pocket.

'Okay,' Dexter said, opening proceedings. 'Welcome to the first briefing for Operation Helix, the investigation into the murder of a young woman who has now been positively identified as Emily Ashcroft, twenty-one years old, of Langham. Emily was at a party at a house on Ketton Road, Upper Hambleton yesterday evening with a number of her friends. At some point we believe to be shortly after midnight, Emily left the property unseen, and was missing until her body was found by a litter picker just before eight o'clock this morning, in a field approximately one hundred and fifty metres behind the house.

'DI Hills and I attended the scene, and also spoke to some of the partygoers, and more statements have been taken by other officers. This opened up a few interesting lines of inquiry. Firstly, we have Liam Carter,' Dexter explained, pointing to Liam's name on the board behind him. 'He's Emily's on-off boyfriend of about a year. He's known to us and has been arrested twice, once for dangerous driving and once for assault on another young man in Cutts Close park in Oakham. Carter was seen pushing Lucy Palmer, Emily's best friend, to the ground following an argument in the garden during last night's party.

'As dodgy as that makes Carter seem, Lucy said that she'd been keeping a close eye on him all night, because she was convinced he was secretly cheating on Emily with another girl who was at the party. After the fight, Liam's mates had taken him off to another part of the house to calm him down and talk some sense into him. Bearing in mind Lucy and Liam's deep dislike of each other, those alibis are solid. She's hardly going to cover for the guy she thinks is cheating on her best mate and who's just physically assaulted her, and there's a party full of witnesses who didn't let Liam out of their sights. Same goes for Lucy – she was with friends the whole time.

'In any case, it feels like Liam Carter might be of interest. Lucy blames him for Emily going off the rails and says he was a bad influence on her. We hear she'd been hanging around with the wrong crowd more recently. An FLO's been out to speak to Emily's parents, who were of a similar opinion. They were less than keen on Liam, and Emily's dad admitted that he'd threatened to cut her out of his will if she didn't stop seeing him. They told us Emily had become very secretive recently, often slipping out late at night and refusing to say where she'd been or who she was with. They said they hadn't seen any evidence of involvement with drugs or criminal activity, but that is a line we should investigate, particularly considering her involvement with Liam Carter.'

Elijah Drummond put his hand up.

'Yes, Elijah,' Dexter said.

'This is all good stuff, but I just wanted to point out that we want to keep all lines of inquiry open. We don't want to focus too heavily on the most tempting routes like Liam Carter, especially if the lad's got multiple solid alibis. We need to make sure we've got our eyes open to all possibilities.'

'Yes, obviously,' Dexter replied, trying desperately not to show his clenched jaw. 'No lines of inquiry are being discounted. I'm simply pointing out the most notable ones at this stage of the investigation.'

Elijah had been a thorn in Dexter's side ever since he'd arrived in Rutland on secondment from EMSOU, the East Midlands Special Operations Unit. It infuriated him that Elijah seemed to think he could waltz in and treat Rutland CID like an incompetent bunch of country bumpkins just because he'd been working in regional Major Crimes. But Dexter suspected there was something darker beneath the surface when it came to Elijah Drummond. He hadn't quite put his finger on what it was yet, but he had a feeling there was far more to the man than met the eye.

'As I was just about to say,' Dexter continued, 'I think we should focus on all aspects of Emily's life. Romantic entanglements aside, you tend to find that it's the parents who have a much better idea of what's going on, despite what the kids might think. We've all been that age, we all know what we got up to, and we all know what to look out for. If we want to see it, that is. Her phone's being checked as we speak, but I'd like us to speak to Emily's parents as soon as possible, so we can get as much background as we can. As always, our focus should be on three things: motive, means and opportunity. Who could have wanted Emily dead, and why? Who was physically able to have committed the offence, and who had the opportunity and window to do it?'

Elijah's hand rose again.

'Go on,' Dexter said.

'The road onto Hambleton was cut off for most of the night because of fallen trees and flooding. So we can discount anyone who wasn't on the peninsula last night, and anyone who wasn't there this morning.'

'We're already aware of that, DS Drummond, thank you. Our list of suspects, essentially, is the list of party guests. Emily wasn't from Hambleton, and she wasn't a regular visitor to Daniel Blackwood's house, nor did she know anyone from Hambleton as far as we're aware. We can tentatively rule out a stranger killing, too, as there were no signs of sexual interference and Emily still had her phone on her, which discounts robbery as a motive. Not to mention the fact that it's extremely unlikely random muggers were walking around Hambleton in the middle of a huge storm.'

'Someone was,' Elijah remarked, this time without raising his hand.

Dexter looked at him for a moment, the atmosphere in the room growing tenser.

'You're absolutely right,' Dexter said eventually, nodding. 'Someone was.'

Caroline pulled up outside what had been Emily Ashcroft's family home in Langham. She was often struck by how the world could seem to go on so easily after the most horrific incidents had occurred, and she looked up at the Ashcroft house, noticing that – from the outside – no-one would ever suspect the tragic news that had befallen its occupants that morning.

Before she could ring the bell, the front door opened.

'Hi, Colin Ashcroft?' Caroline asked.

'Yes,' came the reply.

'Detective Inspector Caroline Hills, from Rutland CID. Is it okay if I come in?'

Colin Ashcroft stepped aside and gestured for Caroline to enter.

Caroline stepped into the hallway, immediately noting the pristine condition of the house. It was immaculate, almost sterile, which somehow made the situation feel even more surreal. Colin led her into a spacious living room, where Emily's mother, Susan, sat on the edge of a sofa, clutching a tissue.

'Please, take a seat,' Colin said, his voice strained but polite.

Caroline nodded and sat down opposite them. She took a moment to observe the couple. Colin's face was tight with barely contained emotion, while Susan's eyes were red from crying, her hands trembling slightly.

'Mr and Mrs Ashcroft, I'm very sorry for your loss,' Caroline began gently. 'I know this is an incredibly difficult time, but we need to ask you some questions to help us understand what happened to Emily.'

Susan nodded, dabbing her eyes with the tissue. 'Yes, of course,' she whispered.

'Can you tell me about Emily's recent behaviour?' Caroline asked. 'Had she seemed different lately? Was there anything worrying her?'

Colin sighed heavily. 'Emily had always been a spirited girl, but recently she'd become more... rebellious. Staying out late, not telling us where she was going, who she was with. We were worried about her.'

'Did she ever mention anyone new in her life?' Caroline probed.

'She was seeing someone,' Colin said, his voice tightening. 'A boy named Liam. We didn't approve.'

'Why not?' Caroline asked.

'He wasn't good enough for her,' Colin replied bluntly.

'He's from a working-class family. No ambition, no future. I told Emily she needed to end it, or we'd cut her off financially.'

Caroline raised an eyebrow. 'You threatened to cut her off?'

'Yes,' Colin admitted, his face hardening. 'It was for her own good. She needed to know we wouldn't support that kind of relationship.'

Caroline glanced at Susan, who looked uncomfortable but didn't contradict her husband. 'Mrs Ashcroft, did you feel the same way about Liam?'

Susan hesitated, then nodded. 'Colin only wanted what was best for Emily. We both did.'

Caroline picked up on the underlying tension. 'It sounds like Emily's relationship with Liam caused a lot of friction in the family.'

'It did,' Colin said sharply. 'She was so stubborn. She wouldn't listen to reason. We were just trying to protect her.'

'Did Emily ever mention feeling threatened or scared?' Caroline asked.

'No, never,' Susan replied quickly. 'She was headstrong, but she never seemed frightened.'

Caroline noted the undertones of dysfunction and classism in the family dynamics. 'Thank you for sharing that with me,' she said. 'I know it's difficult.'

'Do you think Liam had something to do with this?' Colin asked, his voice cracking.

'We're looking into all possibilities,' Caroline said

diplomatically. 'But I need to ask if there's anything else you can tell me about Emily's recent behaviour. Any changes, no matter how small, could be important.'

Colin looked down, his fists clenched. 'She was secretive. Sometimes she'd come home late, looking... dishevelled. I feared she was getting involved in things she shouldn't be.'

'Like what?'

'Drugs, maybe. Or... I don't know. We just didn't know her anymore,' Colin admitted, his voice breaking.

Susan's tears flowed freely now. 'We tried to reach her, but she pushed us away.'

Caroline felt a pang of empathy. 'I understand. Thank you for your honesty. We'll do everything we can to find out what happened to Emily. May I have a look in her room? Sometimes we find clues that might help us understand her better.'

Colin and Susan exchanged a glance before Colin nodded. 'Of course. It's upstairs, second door on the left.'

Caroline made her way up the stairs, the weight of the investigation pressing down on her shoulders. She entered Emily's room, immediately noting how tidy it was. A shelf lined with books and knick-knacks ran along one side of the room. A desk sat by the window, cluttered with notebooks, pens, and a laptop. The bed was neatly made, with a few cushions arranged at the headboard.

Caroline took a moment to take in the atmosphere. The room felt like a snapshot of Emily's life, a blend of youthful enthusiasm and burgeoning independence. She could see hints of Emily's personality in the carefully chosen decor and the eclectic mix of items scattered around.

She began to methodically look through the room, careful not to disturb anything more than necessary. She opened the desk drawers, finding nothing of any particular interest. Nothing seemed immediately out of place.

As she moved to the bookshelf, she noticed a few titles on psychology and self-help, nestled between novels and biographies. One book caught her eye – an old, well-worn journal. She flipped through it briefly, but it seemed to contain only mundane entries about school and friends. She put it back, making a mental note to mention it to the team.

Caroline then approached the wardrobe, opening it to reveal a neatly arranged collection of clothes. She rifled through the hangers, her fingers brushing against the fabric, but found nothing unusual. She crouched down to check the bottom shelves, where a few pairs of shoes were lined up. As she was about to close the door, she caught a glimpse of a small, inconspicuous box tucked away in the corner.

She pulled out the box and opened it to find a collection of keepsakes – ticket stubs, photographs, and small trinkets. It was clear these items held sentimental value, but there was nothing that seemed relevant to the investigation. She carefully placed the box back and stood up, feeling a mix of frustration and determination.

The tension in the room seemed to thicken as she felt

the frustration of a case that seemed to be getting more and more impenetrable by the minute.

7

Caroline drummed her fingers on the steering wheel as she navigated the winding country roads towards Sophie's address. The gentle hum of the engine filled the silence between her and Dexter.

'So, what do we know about Sophie?' Dexter asked, breaking the quiet.

'Not much yet. Environmental Science graduate from the University of Leicester, same as Emily. Currently working for the local council's environmental department.'

Dexter nodded, jotting notes in his pad. 'Bit odd, isn't it? Both of them studying the same subject, working in the same field, then one ends up dead.'

'Let's not jump to conclusions, Dex. But yes, it's certainly interesting.'

They pulled up outside a modest house on the outskirts of Oakham. As they approached the front door, Caroline noticed the neatly tended garden, a sign of a house-proud owner.

Caroline rapped on the door, and after a moment, it swung open to reveal a young woman with tired eyes and tousled brown hair. 'Can I help you?'

'Sophie Trent?' Caroline asked, flashing her warrant card. 'I'm Detective Inspector Caroline Hills, and this is Detective Sergeant Dexter Antoine. We'd like to ask you a few questions about Emily Ashcroft.'

Sophie nodded gently, her eyes welling with tears. 'God, this all makes it seem even more real.'

'May we come in?' Caroline asked gently.

Sophie nodded, stepping aside to let them enter. The inside of the house was as orderly as the outside, with stacks of magazines neatly arranged on a coffee table.

'How well did you know Emily?' Caroline asked as they settled in the living room.

Sophie sniffed, wiping her eyes. 'We'd been friends since uni. We both grew up locally, but we didn't know each other. She went to private schools, and I was at the local state ones, so our paths never crossed. She did Environmental Science at Leicester, same as me, then we both came back after graduation. I got the job with the council, and she... she went to work for a waste management company.'

'Did you keep in touch after university?'

'Of course. We'd meet up for coffee, catch up on gossip. But lately...' Sophie trailed off, her gaze distant.

'Lately?' Dexter prompted.

Sophie sighed. 'She'd been acting strange. Secretive. I thought maybe she'd met someone new, but when I asked, she'd just change the subject.'

Caroline leaned forward, her interest piqued. 'When was the last time you saw her?'

'About a week ago. We met for lunch at that new café on the High Street. She seemed... distracted. Kept checking her phone.'

'Did she mention anything unusual? Any problems at work, perhaps?'

Sophie hesitated, then shook her head. 'Not really. But...'

'But what?' Caroline pressed.

'It's probably nothing, but she did ask me about some old water quality reports. Said it was for a work project, but when I offered to help, she got all cagey about it.'

Caroline and Dexter exchanged a glance. 'And did you give her those reports?'

Sophie nodded. 'Yeah, I mean, they're public record anyway. I just made it easier for her to access them.'

As they wrapped up the interview, Caroline couldn't shake the feeling that they'd just scratched the surface of something much bigger. Emily's secretive behaviour, the water quality reports – it all pointed to something beyond a simple murder case.

'Thank you for your time, Sophie,' Caroline said as they stood to leave. 'We'll be in touch if we need anything else.'

Outside, as they walked back to the car, Dexter voiced

what Caroline was thinking. 'There's more to this than meets the eye, isn't there?'

Caroline nodded grimly. 'Oh yes, Dex. I think there is.'

8

The afternoon sun cast long shadows across the open office as the team gathered around their desks, ready for the briefing. The sound of muted conversations and the occasional rustle of papers filled the air. Dexter stood near the whiteboard, his presence commanding attention. Caroline took a seat at her desk, her notebook at the ready.

'Alright, let's get down to it,' Dexter said, his voice cutting through the low murmur. 'Sara, what have you got on Liam Carter?'

Sara Henshaw adjusted her glasses and glanced at her notes. 'We've done a thorough background check on Liam Carter. He's had a turbulent relationship with Emily, marked by jealousy and aggression. Several witnesses have mentioned seeing him argue with her at various parties over the past few months. One witness, a friend of Emily's, said she overheard them arguing at a house party two weeks ago. Liam was accusing Emily of flirting with other guys. The witness said Liam was visibly upset and was shouting that Emily was making him look like a fool. He was really quite agitated, and it took a couple of friends to calm him down.'

Sara continued, 'Another incident occurred about a month ago. Liam and Emily were at a cocktail bar, Ovation, in Oakham. According to the barmaid, they had a heated argument. Liam was accusing Emily of spending too much time with her male friends. The barmaid had to ask Liam to leave because he was causing a scene and upsetting other patrons.'

Dexter nodded, making a note on the whiteboard. 'We'll need to bring him in for questioning. We need to dig deeper into his behaviour and find out if anyone else witnessed these outbursts. We also need to make sure we get statements from the friend and the barmaid at Ovation.'

Caroline added, 'Rachel also mentioned that Liam has a history of getting aggressive when he drinks. She said he was once kicked out of a club for starting a fight with a guy who was talking to Emily. It seems like his jealousy often turned into aggression. It looks like an established pattern of behaviour.'

'Definitely a strong case for bringing him in and speaking to him under caution,' Dexter replied. 'We've also taken a statement from a friend of Emily's called Sophie Trent. Sophie and Emily met at university, and Sophie now works for the council in their environmental department. She mentioned Emily had been acting strangely recently, and that she'd asked Sophie for access to water quality reports in a way which wasn't usual for her line of work. We're prioritising that as a strong lead, too.'

Caroline listened intently, noting the unease that settled over the team. The room fell silent as the implications of the information sank in.

'So we've got two potential leads,' Dexter said, breaking the silence. 'Liam's jealousy and aggression, and Emily's possible involvement with this whistleblowing. We need to follow up on both.'

DS Elijah Drummond leaned back in his chair, a smirk playing on his lips. 'We should also consider whether Liam might have been onto something. For all we know, Emily could have been having it away with someone else. If she was known to go after bad boys, that guy could be the one we're after.'

Dexter's jaw tightened. 'That's a bit of a stretch, don't you think, Elijah? What about sticking to procedure and not jumping to half-baked theories?'

Elijah's smirk faded slightly, but he held his ground. 'I don't see anything wrong with considering all possibilities, which is what I *actually* said this morning. We can't afford to overlook any angles.'

'Or maybe you're just trying to muddy the waters,' Dexter shot back, his voice low and intense. 'What are your real motives here, Elijah?'

Elijah's eyes narrowed. 'My motive is to find out who

killed Emily Ashcroft. If you think I'm doing anything else, then you're way off the mark.'

Caroline interjected, attempting to lower the tension. 'We should coordinate with forensics to see if we can get any information from Emily's phone.'

Dexter nodded, his expression hardening. 'Yes,' he said, addressing the team and reaffirming his attention. 'I believe that's being worked on as we speak. DI Hills?'

Caroline cleared her throat. 'Well, it's been handed over to digital forensics, who are working on bypassing the PIN. It'll take some time, but once we get in, we should have access to any messages, call logs and other activity on the handset. It could provide us with a clearer picture of her interactions in the days leading up to her death.'

Dexter made a note. 'Good. We'll keep a close eye on that. In the meantime, Sara, I want you to take the lead on bringing Liam in. Aidan, start opening up avenues of investigation into the environmental waste issues.'

The team dispersed, each member with a clear task ahead. The office buzzed with renewed activity, the clatter of keyboards and murmur of conversations filling the air. The investigation was gaining momentum, and Dexter felt a renewed sense of determination. Despite the friction within the team, they were getting closer to the truth, one piece at a time.

9

Caroline was just finishing a call with forensics, jotting down notes as she listened intently. The conversation was about the initial analysis of Emily's phone. While there wasn't much to report yet, it was clear that the phone could be a crucial piece of evidence. The hum of the office around her was a constant reminder of the high stakes they were dealing with.

'Thanks, Mike. Keep me updated,' she said, hanging up and setting her phone down. She glanced at the clock, noting the time. The afternoon was slipping away, and there was still so much to do. She was about to review her notes when Dexter approached, looking slightly frazzled.

'What's up, Dex?' she asked, noting the tension in his shoulders. The creases on his forehead and the tightness around his mouth indicated that he was under significant stress.

Dexter ran a hand through his hair, a gesture she

recognised as a sign something wasn't right. 'I've just had Leah MacGregor from the Rutland & Stamford Mercury on the phone. She's sniffing around for details on the case.'

Caroline raised an eyebrow. Leah MacGregor was known for her tenacity and knack for getting inside scoops before anyone else. She was a big advocate for the public's right to know about local crimes, often sensationalising stories to grab readers' attention. The idea of Leah digging into their investigation was enough to unsettle anyone.

'What did she want?' Caroline asked, leaning back in her chair and crossing her arms.

'Everything,' Dexter replied with a sigh. He leaned against her desk, the weight of the situation evident in his posture. 'She's heard rumours spreading locally and wants confirmation. She's pushing for details on Emily's death, the suspects, and the investigation's progress. I don't want to give her an inch and have her take a mile, but I also don't want her making things up due to a lack of real information.'

Caroline nodded thoughtfully. 'Leah's a tough one. If we don't give her something, she'll fill in the blanks herself, and that could be even worse.' She could imagine the headlines Leah might concoct, each one more sensational than the last, potentially jeopardising their investigation.

Dexter looked at her, his expression a mix of frustration and concern. 'Exactly. We need to be mindful of containing the rumours and dealing with the added scrutiny. How do we handle this?' He rubbed his temples, his eyes betraying the exhaustion he was trying to hide.

Caroline considered the options, her mind racing. 'We could give her a controlled statement. Just enough to satisfy her curiosity without jeopardising the investigation.'

Dexter rubbed his temples again. 'I know we need to say something, but every word she gets will be twisted. She has a way of turning a simple fact into a headline that screams scandal.' His voice was tinged with frustration, the kind that comes from knowing you're in a no-win situation.

Caroline sighed, looking around the bustling office. The hum of conversations and the clatter of keyboards created a backdrop of urgency. 'True, but we can't afford to be silent. Silence breeds speculation, and speculation can derail the investigation. We need to manage the narrative.'

'What should we include?' Dexter asked, clearly relieved to have a plan. His notebook was already open, pen poised, ready to jot down her suggestions.

'First, we acknowledge the public concern. That shows we're not ignoring the issue. Then, we provide basic facts —confirm that Emily's death is under investigation and that we're following multiple leads. Emphasise that it's an active investigation, so we can't disclose too much. We can also stress the importance of not spreading unverified information, as it can hinder our efforts.' Caroline's voice was steady, each word chosen carefully.

Dexter nodded, jotting down notes. 'Right. And what about the suspects? Do we mention Liam or EWMS?'

Caroline shook her head. 'Not by name. We can say we have avenues and persons of interest and are conducting thorough investigations. That way, we don't tip them off or cause unnecessary panic. We should also mention that we're following up on significant new evidence, like the phone we found. It shows progress without giving too much away.'

Dexter seemed to relax a bit, the tension easing from his shoulders. 'That sounds solid. I'll prepare a statement and run it by you before I call her back.'

'Good idea,' Caroline replied. She watched him for a moment, seeing the strain lift slightly from his face. 'And Dex, don't let her bully you into revealing more than we need to. We're in control of this narrative.'

Dexter gave her a grateful smile. 'Thanks. I appreciate the backup and support.'

As Dexter walked back to his desk, Caroline felt a renewed sense of determination. The pressure from the press was just another layer to the complex investigation, but they were making progress. She glanced around the office, the buzz of activity a constant reminder of the stakes. Every officer was deeply engrossed in their tasks. One step at a time, they would uncover the truth behind Emily's death.

Just as she was about to return to her notes, Sara Henshaw hurried over, her face lit with urgency. The gravity in her eyes was palpable, and it made Caroline's heart skip a beat.

'We've managed to get access to Emily's social media accounts,' Sara said, her voice barely containing her excitement. 'There's something there you need to see. I think it's important.'

Caroline and Dexter exchanged a glance, a mixture of anticipation and apprehension hanging in the air. The gravity of Sara's words settled over them like a dense fog, thick with potential revelations.

'Alright,' Dexter said, standing up. 'Let's take a look.'

10

Sara took a deep breath as she relayed her findings to
Dexter and Caroline.

'Okay. So Emily wasn't a massive over-sharer on social
media. That's the first thing to know. Her accounts were
all pretty well locked down, and her Instagram was private
and not open to public view. But there were a couple of
cryptic posts on her Insta feed which indicate some sort of
relationship issues.'

Caroline looked at the screen and the two posts Sara
had highlighted.

> Sometimes the truth is more dangerous
> than the lies we live. #Secrets
> #NotWhatTheySeem

> It's hard to watch someone you care about
> make bad choices. #Heartbreak #Lost

'Okay,' Caroline said. 'Fairly innocuous stuff, but worth bearing in mind.'

'Yup. Agreed. If anything, she comes across as the caring person who's watched someone close to her take the wrong path. Except, when I looked at her private messages, there's a short conversation with another user called "chazclarets05" two days before that last post about watching someone you care about making bad choices. Have a look.'

> Heyyy, a mutual said you might be able to help me out? ❄️

> Hey... ask them for my telegram - not here 👍

'Drugs,' Dexter said immediately. 'The snowflake emoji's a reference to cocaine.'

'Do we know that for certain, though?' Caroline asked. 'We don't want to jump to conclusions.'

'I agree, but I think we can be 95% sure, at the very least. Why else would she refuse to discuss it there and want to move to Telegram?'

Caroline gave him a blank look. 'I don't know. Why?'

'Because Telegram's a totally secure messaging service. You've got terrorist organisations using it for communications, never mind low level drug dealers.'

'But we don't know Emily *was* dealing. All we know is that someone sent her a vague message about helping them out, and she wanted to move to a different app.'

'It fits the general pattern with these sorts of things,' Sara interjected. 'I'd be inclined to agree with Dex.'

Caroline nodded. 'Alright. It's definitely well worth looking into. How do we track down this other user and find out who it is?'

'We can put in a request to Instagram to release any information they have,' Dexter said. 'But our best hope is likely to be Emily's phone. If we can manage to get that unlocked, we'll have access to all her message history on Telegram.'

'Do we have any news on that?' Caroline asked.

'Not yet. But we're hoping for an update soon.'

'There is one other thing,' Sara said, having waited patiently for her chance to speak. 'I took the liberty of looking through Emily's Facebook friends list. One name stood out to me – Charlie Holbanks. I think he's "chazclarets05".'

'What makes you think that?' Caroline asked.

'Well, obviously the "Chaz" bit is what got me started. And when you click onto Charlie's profile…' Sara said, as she did so. 'You can see a good chunk of his posts are about Burnley Football Club. Otherwise known as the Clarets. And if you go onto his information section… There you go.'

'Born in 2005,' Caroline said, her voice almost a whisper. 'Brilliant work, Sara. You might be right. Let's get an address for Charlie Holbanks. I think we need to have a word and see what he knows.'

'Will do. And for our finale, Emily's Facebook

messages. All pretty innocuous apart from one that stood out: a conversation with someone called Ashley Bignell, who was one of Emily's work colleagues. Ashley messaged Emily a week ago, asking if she was okay because she'd seen their boss shouting at Emily at work. Emily says she's fine, and that it was just a misunderstanding, and the conversation peters out there. It might be nothing, but Ashley obviously thought it was serious enough to find Emily on Facebook and send her a message to check she was alright. There's no other conversation history between them.'

Dexter raised his eyebrows. 'Presumably this is the same job Sophie Trent was talking about, with the water reports?'

'I'm assuming so,' Sara replied. 'That's the employer listed on her profile.'

'Good work. Think we'd better get that kettle on,' Dexter said. 'Looks like we've got plenty to be getting on with.'

11

Dexter pulled into the car park, the morning sun casting long shadows across the asphalt. The gates creaked open as he drove through, the familiar sound doing little to ease the knot of tension in his stomach. As he entered, he immediately spotted two familiar figures standing just inside the gates, near the entrance. Elijah was speaking animatedly with Leah MacGregor, the local newspaper reporter known for her tenacity and penchant for scandalous headlines. Dexter's stomach tightened further. Leah shouldn't even be inside the gates – this was restricted access, and Elijah knew better.

He drove past them slowly, trying to gauge their conversation without being obvious. Leah's notepad was out, her pen poised as Elijah gestured animatedly. Dexter's mind raced. *What is he telling her?* He continued driving, finding a parking spot a little further away. He turned off the engine and sat for a moment, gripping the steering wheel tightly. He watched them in his rear-view mirror, his thoughts a whirlwind of frustration and concern.

I can't stay in the car forever, he thought. *That'll look suspicious*. He needed to act quickly but carefully. Taking a deep breath, Dexter reminded himself to stay calm. He couldn't afford to let his emotions get the better of him. He opened the car door and stepped out, the cool morning air hitting him like a splash of cold water.

With each step towards them, the knot in his stomach grew tighter. He forced a smile onto his face as he approached. 'Morning, Leah. Elijah,' he said, his voice steady. 'I was planning to have an official response with you later this morning, Leah.'

Leah turned to face him, her eyes gleaming with anticipation. 'I needed something sooner, DS Antoine. We've got print deadlines to meet. Besides which, it's in the public interest to know what's going on.'

Dexter nodded, trying to keep his frustration in check. 'I understand, but it's important we manage the flow of information carefully. We don't want to jeopardise the investigation.'

Elijah stood there with a smug expression, clearly enjoying Dexter's discomfort. 'Leah was just asking a few questions, mate. No harm in that, right? Besides which, you seem to forget I've done this hundreds of times before with EMSOU.'

Dexter felt a surge of anger but knew he needed to keep his composure. He could tell from the look on Leah's face that she was enjoying every second of this. He dreaded to think what salacious gossip she might come up with now. He could almost see the headlines.

USELESS COPS MORE INTERESTED IN ARGUING THAN CATCHING CRIMINALS.

Confronting them directly could backfire and create an even bigger issue. He couldn't afford to let Elijah and Leah get the better of him.

'Of course,' Dexter replied, his tone measured. 'We'll have an *official* statement over to you this morning. I presume that's not too late for your print deadline?'

Leah looked at him for a moment before smiling. 'No. That'll be absolutely fine.'

'Great. Have a good day.' He turned to walk into the building, feeling Leah's eyes on his back.

Inside, the tension still hung over him like a dark cloud. What had Elijah told her? How much damage control would he need to do? When it came to Elijah Drummond, it felt as if all Dexter ever did was damage control. His thoughts raced as he made his way to the briefing room.

The team was already gathering inside. The atmosphere was tense, everyone sensing the urgency and high stakes of the case. Caroline sat at her desk, tapping away on her computer. Her office door was wide open, displaying her role as his boss, mentor and confidant, whilst at the same time giving him the space to head up his own investigation.

Dexter tried to push the encounter with Leah and Elijah out of his mind. He needed to focus on the investigation. The morning briefing would bring its own set of challenges, and he had to be ready.

He walked over to Caroline and cleared his throat. 'I just saw Leah MacGregor speaking with Elijah outside in the car park.'

Caroline's eyes widened. 'Are you joking?'

'Not in the slightest. He'll be here in a minute. This conversation didn't happen.'

Dexter took his position at the front of the room and began the morning briefing immediately, without waiting for Elijah.

Caroline got up from her desk and came into the main room, watching on.

After a couple of minutes, Elijah sauntered into the room with a steaming mug of coffee in his hand. He stopped and paused for a moment, before looking at his watch.

'We starting early?' he asked, before sitting down at his desk.

'We were all ready, Elijah,' Dexter replied. 'It's a shame you weren't, but we've got important matters to be getting on with.'

The thing Dexter noticed most was that Elijah gave no discernible response to this. His face was still, stoic.

As the briefing continued, Dexter felt a mixture of frustration and determination. He couldn't let Elijah's antics derail the investigation.

The briefing wrapped up, and tasks had been assigned, ensuring everyone was clear on their objectives for the day. Dexter's mind was already racing with plans to follow up on leads and gather more evidence. But he couldn't shake the lingering tension. The encounter with Leah and Elijah had set a tone for the day, and he knew he had to stay focused and vigilant. The investigation was far from over, and there was no room for distractions.

He headed to his desk, ready to dive into the day's work and, hopefully, focus his mind on something else. The case was complex, with many threads to unravel, but he was determined to see it through.

He knew what Elijah's game was, and he wasn't having any of it. He'd had enough of bullies in his life, and he wasn't about to give in to his gaslighting and devious antics. No matter what obstacles Elijah threw in his path, he would stay the course. Emily's family deserved nothing less.

12

Aidan pulled into the car park of Environmental Waste Management Solutions, the company's stark logo looming over him as he stepped out of his car. The grey sky and drizzling rain seemed fitting for the sombre mood that hung over the investigation.

As he approached the entrance, Aidan couldn't help but feel a twinge of unease. Something about this place felt off, though he couldn't quite put his finger on what. He pushed the thought aside, focusing on the task at hand.

The receptionist, a young woman with a forced smile, directed him to a small meeting room. 'Ashley will be with you shortly,' she said, her voice barely above a whisper.

Aidan nodded his thanks and settled into an uncomfortable plastic chair. He drummed his fingers on the table, his mind racing through the questions he needed to ask. The team briefings had provided some context, but he knew there was more to uncover.

The door opened, and a woman in her early thirties entered. Her dark hair was pulled back in a neat bun, and her eyes were rimmed with red, as if she'd been crying recently.

'Ashley Bignell?' Aidan asked, standing to greet her.

She nodded, shaking his outstretched hand. 'Yes, that's me. You're here about Emily, aren't you?'

Aidan gestured for her to sit. 'I'm Detective Constable Aidan Chilcott. I'm investigating Emily Ashcroft's death, and I was hoping you could answer a few questions for me.'

Ashley sank into the chair opposite him, her shoulders slumped. 'Of course. It's just... I can't believe she's gone. We weren't close friends or anything, but still...'

'I understand,' Aidan said, his tone gentle. 'These situations are never easy. Can you tell me about your working relationship with Emily?'

Ashley took a deep breath. 'Well, I'm in admin so I tend to work with people across departments. She was always friendly, always had a smile for everyone. It's hard to imagine anyone wanting to hurt her.'

Aidan nodded, jotting down notes. 'Did you notice any changes in Emily's behaviour recently? Anything out of the ordinary?'

Ashley hesitated, her fingers fidgeting with the hem of her blouse. 'Well, there was... I'm not sure if it's important, but...'

'Anything you can tell us could be helpful,' Aidan encouraged.

'There was an argument,' Ashley said, her voice lowering. 'Between Emily and Philip Grayson, one of the directors. It was about a week ago.'

Aidan leaned forward, his interest piqued. 'Can you tell me more about that? What was the argument about?'

Ashley glanced towards the door, as if worried someone might overhear. 'I didn't catch all of it, but Philip seemed really angry. He was accusing Emily of accessing files she shouldn't have, of taking them off-site.'

'Did you hear Emily's response?'

Ashley shook her head. 'She was speaking too quietly for me to hear. But she looked... scared. I'd never seen her like that before.'

Aidan made a note, his mind racing with the implications. 'Do you know what kind of files they were talking about?'

'No, sorry,' Ashley replied. 'We deal with a lot of sensitive information here, but I don't know the specifics of what Emily was working on.'

Aidan nodded, trying to keep his expression neutral despite his growing suspicion. 'Did you notice anything else unusual about Emily's behaviour after that argument?'

Ashley furrowed her brow, thinking. 'She was quieter, I suppose. Kept to herself more. And she was staying late a lot, which wasn't like her. She usually left on time to meet her boyfriend.'

'Liam Carter?' Aidan asked, recalling the name from previous briefings.

'That's right,' Ashley confirmed. 'She used to talk

about him sometimes. They seemed happy, but...' She trailed off, looking uncertain.

'But what?' Aidan prompted.

Ashley sighed. 'I don't know. Maybe I'm reading too much into things, but the last few weeks, she didn't mention him as much. And when she did, she seemed... I don't know, sad? Worried? It's hard to explain.'

Aidan made another note. 'Is there anything else you can tell me about Emily's work here? Any projects she was particularly invested in?'

Ashley shook her head. 'I'm sorry, I don't know much about the specifics of her work. We're all pretty compartmentalised here. Security protocols and all that.'

Aidan nodded, sensing he wasn't going to get much more from Ashley. 'Thank you for your time, Miss Bignell. You've been very helpful. If you think of anything else, no matter how small it might seem, please don't hesitate to contact us. I, uh, don't suppose Philip Grayson's in today, is he?'

'He's not, actually,' Ashley replied. 'I think he's back in tomorrow, though.'

'Not to worry,' Aidan said, smiling.

As he stood to leave, Ashley spoke up again. 'Detective? I hope you find whoever did this to Emily. She... she didn't deserve this.'

Aidan gave her a reassuring smile. 'We're doing everything we can to get to the truth. Thank you again for your help.'

As he walked back to his car, Aidan's mind was

whirling with new information. The argument with the boss, the confidential files, Emily's changed behaviour... It all pointed to something bigger going on. He couldn't shake the feeling that they were just scratching the surface of a much larger issue.

He slid into the driver's seat, pulling out his phone to update Caroline. As he dialled, he glanced back at the EWMS building. Something was definitely not right here, and he was determined to find out what it was.

13

Dexter pulled up outside the modest semi-detached house, the car's engine ticking as it cooled. He glanced at Sara, noting the determined set of her jaw.

'Ready?' he asked.

Sara nodded, her eyes fixed on the house. 'Let's do this.'

They approached the front door, treading carefully on the cracked concrete path. The overgrown garden hinted at neglect, matching the peeling paint on the window frames. Dexter knocked firmly, the sound echoing in the quiet street.

After a moment, the door creaked open, revealing a woman in her fifties with worry lines etched deeply into her face. Her eyes darted nervously between them.

'Mrs Holbanks?' Dexter asked. At her nod, he continued, 'I'm Detective Sergeant Antoine, and this is Detective Constable Henshaw.' They both showed their warrant cards. 'We'd like to speak with Charlie, please. Is he home?'

Janet Holbanks' hand tightened on the door frame. 'What's this about?'

Sara stepped in, her voice gentle but professional. 'We're conducting an investigation and believe Charlie might have some information that could assist us. We'd just like to ask him a few questions.'

Janet's eyes narrowed slightly. 'An investigation into what?'

Dexter exchanged a glance with Sara before responding. 'It's regarding a serious incident that occurred recently. We'd prefer to discuss the details inside, if that's alright.'

Janet hesitated, then called over her shoulder, 'Charlie! There are some police officers here to see you.'

They heard shuffling from inside the house, and a moment later, Charlie appeared behind his mother. He was tall and lanky, with disheveled hair and dark circles under his eyes. His gaze immediately dropped to the floor when he saw Dexter and Sara.

'Can we come in?' Dexter asked, his tone polite but firm.

Janet stepped aside reluctantly, ushering them into a cramped hallway. Family photos lined the walls, their frames slightly askew. Charlie retreated to the living room, his mother close behind him.

The living room was small and cluttered, with mismatched furniture and faded wallpaper. Charlie perched on the edge of an armchair, his leg bouncing nervously. Janet hovered nearby, her arms crossed tightly over her chest.

Dexter and Sara sat on the worn sofa opposite Charlie. The springs creaked under their weight, adding to the tension in the room.

'Charlie,' Dexter began, his voice calm and measured, 'we're here to talk about Emily Ashcroft.'

At the mention of Emily's name, Charlie's head snapped up, his eyes wide. Janet inhaled sharply.

'Emily?' Charlie stammered. 'What... what about her?'

Sara leaned forward slightly. 'We're investigating her death, Charlie. We believe you might have some information that could help us understand what happened to her.'

Janet interjected, her voice sharp with worry. 'My Charlie's a good boy. He wouldn't have anything to do with—'

'Mum, please,' Charlie muttered, his cheeks flushing.

Dexter glanced between them, noting the tension. 'Mrs Holbanks, we're not accusing Charlie of anything. We're just trying to gather information. However, it might be easier if we could speak to Charlie alone.'

Janet's face tightened. 'I'm not leaving my son alone with you. He's done nothing wrong.'

Charlie's shoulders hunched further. 'It's okay, Mum. You can go.'

After a moment of tense silence, Janet reluctantly left

the room, though Dexter noticed she didn't go far, hovering just outside the doorway.

'Charlie,' Sara said softly, 'we know you sent Emily a message on Instagram recently. Can you tell us about that?'

Charlie's hands twisted in his lap, his knuckles white. 'It was stupid,' he mumbled. 'I just... I heard she might know where to get some stuff. But she said no. That was it.'

'What kind of stuff, Charlie?' Dexter pressed gently.

Charlie's eyes darted to the doorway where his mother lurked. He lowered his voice. 'Just... you know. Party stuff. Nothing hard. I swear.'

'It's alright,' Dexter said, his voice low. 'We're not interested in pursuing anything like that. We just want to find out what happened to Emily.'

'Yeah. Yeah, I get it,' Charlie replied.

Dexter nodded, keeping his expression neutral. 'And that was the extent of your relationship with Emily?'

'Yeah,' Charlie said quickly. 'We weren't close or anything. Just saw her at parties sometimes.'

'When was the last time you saw her?' Sara asked.

Charlie bit his lip, his brow furrowing in concentration. 'Maybe... two weeks ago? At a house party. I can't remember whose house it was.'

'And did you notice anything unusual about Emily that night?' Dexter inquired.

Charlie hesitated, his leg bouncing faster. 'She seemed... off. Nervous, like.'

'Nervous how?' Sara pressed.

'Just... jumpy. Kept looking over her shoulder, like she thought someone was watching her.'

Dexter and Sara exchanged a glance. 'Did she mention anyone by name? Anyone who might have been causing her concern?'

Charlie shook his head. 'No, but...' he trailed off, biting his lip.

'But what, Charlie?' Dexter encouraged. 'Anything you can tell us could be important.'

Charlie took a deep breath. 'She said something about a guy from out of town. Someone new. The way she talked about him... I got the feeling he was bad news.'

As Charlie spoke, Janet reappeared in the doorway, her face pale. 'Charlie, what are you talking about? You never told me any of this.'

Charlie flinched at his mother's voice. 'I didn't think it was important, Mum. I didn't want you to worry.'

'Do you remember anything else about this man?' Sara asked, redirecting Charlie's attention. 'Did Emily mention a name, or describe him at all?'

Charlie shook his head. 'No, sorry. She didn't say much. Just that he was older, I think. And that he scared her.'

The tension in the room was palpable. Dexter stood, sensing they'd got all they could for now. 'Thank you, Charlie. You've been very helpful. We'll be in touch if we need anything else.'

As they prepared to leave, Janet followed them to the

door, her earlier hostility replaced by fear. 'You'll let us know if you find out anything, won't you?' she asked, her voice trembling. 'About what happened to Emily?'

Dexter nodded solemnly. 'Of course, Mrs Holbanks. Thank you for your cooperation. If either of you remember anything else, no matter how small it might seem, please don't hesitate to contact us.'

Back in the car, Sara turned to Dexter. 'What do you think?'

Dexter sighed, starting the engine. 'I really don't know what to think.'

'Do you believe Charlie?' Sara asked, her brow furrowed.

Dexter drummed his fingers on the steering wheel. 'I think he was holding something back. Did you notice how he kept looking at his mum? I reckon there's more to this than he's letting on.'

Sara nodded. 'Agreed. And this new guy... it's the first we're hearing of him. We need to find out who he is.'

As they drove away, Dexter couldn't shake the image of Charlie's frightened eyes, or the protective fury of his mother. This case was far from over, and he had a feeling it was about to get a lot more complicated.

'Let's head back to the station,' he said. 'We need to update the team and start digging into this new lead. Someone out there knows who this mystery man is, and we're going to find him.'

14

Dexter stared at his phone, Leah MacGregor's number glowing on the screen. He'd been putting off this call, but he knew he couldn't delay any longer. The weight of the investigation pressed down on him, each new lead seeming to raise more questions than answers. With a resigned sigh, he hit the dial button.

'Leah MacGregor,' came the brisk answer after two rings.

'Leah, it's Detective Sergeant Antoine,' Dexter said, keeping his tone professional despite his unease. 'I'm calling with that update I promised.'

'Ah, DS Antoine,' Leah replied, a hint of eagerness in her voice. 'I was beginning to think you'd forgotten about me.'

Dexter could almost hear the smile in her voice, and it set his teeth on edge. He recalled their encounter in the car park, the way she'd seemed to materialise out of thin air, hungry for information. 'We've been rather busy with the investigation,' he said carefully.

'I'm sure you have,' Leah said. 'So, what can you tell me?'

Dexter paused, choosing his words carefully. He glanced at the screen in front of him, his eyes skimming over the photos of Emily Ashcroft, the timeline they'd constructed, the list of potential suspects. 'We're making progress in the investigation into Emily Ashcroft's death. We've interviewed several key witnesses and are following up on promising leads.'

There was a moment of silence on the other end of the line. When Leah spoke again, her voice had lost its friendly edge. 'Come on. You can do better than that. Give me something I can actually use.'

Dexter felt his jaw clench. This was exactly why he disliked dealing with reporters. They always wanted more, never satisfied with the scraps of information he could safely provide. 'I'm afraid I can't disclose any specific details that might compromise the investigation.'

'Alright, let me help you out then,' Leah said, her tone shifting to something more calculating. 'I know you're interested in Environmental Waste Management Solutions. Am I right in thinking Emily Ashcroft was an employee there?'

Dexter felt a jolt of surprise, quickly followed by suspicion. How had she got hold of that information? He thought back to their briefings, trying to recall if they'd mentioned the company in any public statements. 'Ms MacGregor, I can't comment on—'

'So that's a yes, then,' Leah interrupted. 'And I'm guessing there are some connections you're looking into. Care to elaborate?'

Dexter's mind raced. Leah was dangerously close to the truth, and he needed to tread carefully. The image of Aidan's notes from his interview at EWMS flashed through his mind. 'As I said, I can't disclose specifics about an ongoing investigation. Any connections we may or may not be exploring are confidential at this stage.'

'Come on,' Leah pressed. 'You must have something for me. A quote, perhaps? "Police are investigating possible links between the victim's employment and her untimely death." How's that?'

'Ms MacGregor,' Dexter said, struggling to keep his tone even, 'I appreciate your interest in this case, but I must insist that you refrain from speculating or publishing unverified information. It could seriously hamper our investigation.'

Leah's laugh was short and sharp. 'You should know by now that asking a journalist not to speculate is like asking a fish not to swim. If you won't give me anything concrete, I'll have to work with what I've got.'

Dexter felt a headache building behind his eyes. He glanced at the clock on the wall, acutely aware of how much time this call was taking away from the actual investigation. 'I understand you have a job to do, but so do we. And our job is to find justice for Emily Ashcroft. Premature publication of unconfirmed details could jeopardise that.'

'And the public's right to know?' Leah challenged.

'The public's right to know doesn't supersede our duty to conduct a thorough and non-compromised investigation,' Dexter countered. He thought of Emily's parents, their grief-stricken faces when they'd been told about their daughter's death. 'We owe it to the victim and her family to get this right. Publishing incorrect information could result in a killer walking free. Do you really want to be responsible for that?'

There was a pause, and Dexter could almost hear Leah weighing her options. Finally, she spoke again, her voice cooler. 'Alright. I'll hold off for now. But I expect a more substantial update soon. Don't make me dig deeper on my own.'

'I'll keep you informed of any developments we can safely disclose,' Dexter promised, though the words left a bitter taste in his mouth. He knew Leah well enough by now to realise this was far from over.

'See that you do,' Leah said. 'Oh, and DS Antoine? You might want to look into some of EWMS's recent practices. Just a friendly tip.' Before Dexter could respond, the line went dead.

Dexter stared at his phone for a moment, a mix of frustration and unease churning in his stomach. Leah's parting words echoed in his mind. What did she know about EWMS's practices? And more importantly, how did she know it?

He turned to his computer, fingers flying over the keyboard as he pulled up what information they had on the company. Most of it was standard corporate stuff – annual reports, press releases about new contracts. Nothing that immediately screamed 'suspicious'. But Leah's tip, combined with what Aidan had learned from his interview, suggested there was more beneath the surface.

After ending the call, Dexter sat back in his chair, rubbing his temples. He needed to update Caroline immediately. If Leah had somehow got wind of the EWMS connection, who knew what else she might uncover?

He picked up his phone again, dialling Caroline's number. As it rang, he couldn't shake the feeling they were racing against time – not just to solve the case, but to do so before Leah MacGregor blew it wide open in the press. The pressure was mounting, and Dexter knew that one wrong move could send the whole investigation crashing down around them.

Caroline's voicemail picked up, and Dexter left a brief message asking her to call him back urgently. As he set the phone down, his gaze fell on the photo of Emily Ashcroft pinned to the incident board. Her smiling face seemed to watch him, a silent reminder of why they were pushing so hard.

With renewed determination, Dexter turned back to

his computer. They needed to dig deeper into Environmental Waste Management Solutions, and fast. As he began to type out a request for more detailed financial records, he couldn't shake the feeling that they were on the verge of uncovering something big.

15

'Got a minute?' Sara asked, poking her head around Caroline's office door.

Caroline looked up from her desk, where she and Dexter had been going over case notes. 'What is it?'

'Digital forensics is back,' Sara said, holding up her laptop. 'I've been through it, and there's something you need to see.'

Caroline and Dexter exchanged glances. 'Come in,' Caroline said, gesturing to a chair.

Sara sat down and opened the laptop. 'So, we've got access to Emily's phone. Looks like she kept it pretty clean and tidy. She had a habit of deleting old conversations.'

'That's not exactly helpful,' Dexter said, frowning.

'No,' Sara agreed, 'but her calendar is interesting. There are entries that read "Meet K ♥" on quite a few dates.'

'K?' Caroline asked.

Sara nodded. 'Yeah. And here's where it gets more intriguing. We've got details of her phone's cell site data, and on those dates and times she was visiting the home of a Kevin Hartley.'

'Who's Kevin Hartley?' Dexter asked.

Sara turned her laptop around, showing them a spreadsheet. 'I cross-referenced the calendar entries with Emily's location data. Every time there was a "Meet K" entry, her phone pinged near this address.' She pointed to a column on the screen. 'I looked up the electoral roll for that address, and it came back as Kevin Hartley, age forty-nine.'

'Good work,' Caroline nodded. 'So what's the connection?'

'That took a bit more digging,' Sara admitted. 'I searched for his name online and found quite a few references to him being a top environmental lawyer.'

A heavy silence fell over the room. Caroline broke it. 'Right. Let's not jump to conclusions. What else do we know about these meetings?'

'They were regular,' Sara said. 'Usually twice a week, always at his house. The pattern started about three months before Emily's death.'

'Any messages between them?' Dexter asked.

Sara shook her head. 'That's the thing. Emily seems to have been in the habit of deleting her message threads regularly. We couldn't recover anything substantial.'

'Convenient,' Caroline muttered.

'I did find something else, though,' Sara added, clicking through to another screen. 'Emily's browser history shows she'd been looking up information on environmental lawyers in the region. It seems she was shopping around before settling on Hartley.'

Dexter leaned in, squinting at the screen. 'Any idea why she chose him over the others?'

Sara shrugged. 'He's local, and if what's written online is anything to go by, he's bloody good at his job.'

'Might explain why someone fresh out of uni could afford regular appointments,' Caroline mused.

'There could be other reasons she wasn't paying,' Aidan offered. 'If it was some sort of whistleblowing stuff, he might have taken it on pro bono, or offered her a couple of hours a week free of charge.'

Caroline's eyebrows bounced before settling back into place. 'I'm sure he did. In any case, we need to speak to this Kevin Hartley. Dexter, you and Sara head over to his place. See what he has to say about these appointments.'

Dexter nodded. 'What about his alibi for the night Emily died?'

'Good point,' Caroline replied. 'Aidan, can you check that out? See where his phone was pinging that night.'

'On it,' Aidan said, turning back to his computer.

'And Aidan,' Caroline added, 'look into Emily's known associates. See if there's anyone else who might have been spending time with her regularly.'

As Dexter and Sara prepared to leave, Caroline called out. 'Dexter.'

He turned back. 'Yeah?'

'Tread carefully with Hartley. If he's involved, we don't want to spook him. But if he's innocent...'

Dexter nodded, understanding. 'We don't want to ruin his life over a misunderstanding. Got it.'

'And Sara,' Caroline added, 'good work on connecting those dots. Keep digging into Emily's digital footprint. There might be more we're missing.'

As the team dispersed to their tasks, Caroline turned back to the incident board. Emily's smiling photo stared back at her. 'What were you mixed up in?' she murmured to herself, the pieces of the puzzle refusing to fit together neatly.

A young woman, a middle-aged lawyer, and a mystery man from out of town. Somewhere in this tangle of relationships lay the key to Emily's death. She just had to find it.

Caroline sighed, rubbing her temples. Cases involving young victims always hit hard, but this one was proving particularly complex. She glanced at her watch, realising she'd missed lunch again. As she reached for her phone to order a sandwich, it buzzed with a message from Mark.

'Don't forget, parents' evening tonight. I can go alone if you're stuck at work.'

Caroline groaned inwardly. She'd completely forgotten. She quickly typed back: 'I'll be there. Might be a few minutes late.'

Putting her phone down, she took another look at the incident board. Kevin Hartley's name now occupied a prominent space, connected to Emily's with a line and a question mark. Caroline couldn't shake the feeling that this new lead was about to open a can of worms.

16

A couple of hours later, Dexter and Caroline sat in her office, finalising their interview plan for Kevin Hartley.

Uniformed officers had picked Hartley up from his workplace an hour earlier. He'd agreed to come in voluntarily – most likely to avoid causing a scene at work.

Inside the interview room, Kevin Hartley sat calmly, his hands folded on the table. He was a man in his late forties, with salt-and-pepper hair and sharp, intelligent eyes behind wire-rimmed glasses.

'Mr Hartley,' Caroline began as they sat down. 'Thank you for coming in. I'm DI Hills, and this is DS Antoine. We'd like to ask you some questions about Emily Ashcroft.'

Hartley nodded. 'Of course. Although I'm not sure how much help I can be. I didn't really know her well.'

Dexter leaned forward slightly. 'Mr Hartley, we have reason to believe you met with Emily Ashcroft several times over the past few months. Can you explain the nature of these meetings?'

A look of confusion crossed Hartley's face. 'I'm sorry, but there must be some mistake.'

'We have evidence of regular meetings between Emily and someone she referred to as "K",' Caroline pressed. 'On these specific dates.' She slid a sheet of paper across the table.

Hartley glanced at the dates, then chuckled to himself. 'Is that it? You think this is me, because my name begins with a K?'

'Can you explain where you were on these dates, Mr Hartley?' Caroline asked.

Hartley let out a sigh, then looked back at the paper.

'Well, I wasn't even in the country on that day,' he said, jabbing his finger at a line of text. 'And I'm pretty sure this one was the week I was down in Cornwall with work. Yes, it was. The May one… Difficult to say without checking my diary, but it seems about right for the three days I was on an oil rig off the coast of Aberdeen, working with a drilling company on environmental safety compliance.'

'Are you able to prove your whereabouts on these dates?' Caroline asked.

'Absolutely, yes. I'll need to cross-check my diary, but I can assure you I know nothing about any secret meet-ups with Emily Ashcroft. It's a terrible business, what happened, but you're well wide of the mark here.'

Caroline felt a wave of frustration wash over her. Another dead end. 'You're certain about this?'

'Absolutely,' Hartley replied, reaching for his briefcase. 'I always keep meticulous records. I'm a lawyer.'

As the interview concluded, Caroline fought to keep her disappointment from showing. 'Thank you for your time, Mr Hartley. We appreciate your cooperation.'

Outside the interview room, Dexter ran a hand through his hair. 'Well, that was unexpected. Back to square one, I suppose.'

'Yeah,' Caroline replied, sighing. 'Seems that way.'

17

Dexter shouldered his bag and headed for the exit. The office was quiet, most of the team having left for the day. As he pushed open the heavy fire door, the cool evening air hit his face. He paused, fishing in his pocket for his car keys.

A flicker of movement caught his eye. Elijah was leaning against his car, tapping away at his mobile phone. Dexter's jaw clenched involuntarily. With no one else around, he decided it was time to clear the air.

'Elijah,' he called out, striding towards him. 'Got a minute?'

Elijah looked up, his face betraying a flicker of surprise before settling into a neutral expression. 'Sure, what's up?'

Dexter stopped a few feet away, hands in his pockets. 'Look, I know what you've been up to. The business with Leah MacGregor? It stops now.'

Elijah's eyebrows rose. 'I'm not sure what you mean.'

'Don't play dumb,' Dexter said, his voice low. 'You're new here. You don't know how we do things. But undermining your colleagues? That's not on.'

A smirk played at the corner of Elijah's mouth. 'Undermining? Is that what you call it when someone actually does their job properly?'

Dexter felt his face grow hot. 'What's that supposed to mean?'

Elijah pushed himself off the car, standing up straight. 'It means some of us don't get distracted by football memorabilia when there's a killer on the loose.'

Dexter froze. It was obvious what Elijah was referring to. Three years earlier, Dexter had a momentary lapse of concentration, allowing a potential suspect out of his sight for just long enough to destroy crucial CCTV evidence. As a result, another person had lost their life.

'Who told you about that?' Dexter demanded, taking a step closer.

Elijah's smirk widened. 'Does it matter? The fact is, your little lapse in judgement cost a man his life. Jack Hayward, wasn't it?'

Dexter's mind raced. While the team knew about his mistake, Elijah was new. Someone must have filled him in, but who? And why?

'You're out of line,' Dexter growled, struggling to keep his voice steady.

'Am I?' Elijah countered. 'Or are you just afraid someone might realise you're not cut out for this job?'

Dexter's fists clenched at his sides. He wanted nothing

more than to wipe that smug look off Elijah's face. But he knew he couldn't. Not here, not now.

'You don't know what you're talking about,' Dexter said, forcing himself to take a step back. 'And if you've got any sense, you'll drop this now.'

Elijah shrugged, reaching for his car door. 'Whatever you say, boss. Just remember, some of us are here to solve crimes, not admire sports memorabilia.'

As Elijah moved to open his car door, Dexter's hand shot out, slamming it shut. The metallic thud echoed across the empty car park.

'We're not done here,' Dexter said, his voice dangerously low. 'You want to throw accusations around? Fine. But you'd better be damn sure you know what you're talking about.'

Elijah's eyes narrowed. 'Oh, I know exactly what I'm talking about. You got distracted, Fletcher slipped away, destroyed the evidence, and because of that, a killer stayed free long enough to claim another victim. Those are the facts, aren't they?'

Dexter felt a cold weight settle in his stomach. The guilt he'd been carrying for three years threatened to overwhelm him. 'You weren't there,' he managed. 'You don't know the circumstances.'

'I know enough,' Elijah shot back. 'I know that in this job, a moment's lapse can have dire consequences. And I know that some people aren't equipped to handle that responsibility.'

Dexter's grip on the car door tightened. 'And you think

you are? You've been here five minutes. You don't know the first thing about—'

'I know how to stay focused on the job,' Elijah interrupted. 'I know how to put the victims first, instead of getting starstruck by a bit of sports tat.'

The accusation hit Dexter like a physical blow. He stepped back, his hand falling away from the car door. 'Who told you about this?' he asked, his voice barely above a whisper.

Elijah opened his car door, pausing before he got in. 'Does it matter? The whole team knows. I'm just the only one willing to call you out on it.'

As Elijah climbed into his car, Dexter stood rooted to the spot, a mixture of anger and paranoia swirling in his gut. Who had filled Elijah in on the details? And why? Was someone trying to undermine him?

He watched Elijah's taillights disappear into the gathering darkness, the weight of his guilt and fear pressing down on him like a physical force. One thing was certain: this wasn't over.

Dexter walked back to his own car, his mind racing. Had someone in the office been talking behind his back? Or worse, was there a concerted effort to push him out?

As he slid into the driver's seat, Dexter's phone buzzed. A text from Caroline.

> Everything okay? You're usually gone by now.

Dexter stared at the message, his thumb hovering over

the keyboard. Should he tell her about Elijah? About the confrontation?

After a moment's hesitation, he typed out a reply.

> All fine. Just finishing up some paperwork.
> See you tomorrow.

He tossed the phone onto the passenger seat and started the engine. As he pulled out of the car park, Dexter couldn't shake the feeling that things were about to get a lot more complicated. There was someone on the team he couldn't trust.

18

Aidan took a deep breath as he stood outside Philip
Grayson's office at Environmental Waste Management
Solutions. The sleek, modern building felt cold and
impersonal, a stark contrast to the weight of the task
ahead. He knocked firmly on the door.

'Come in,' a gruff voice called from inside.

Aidan entered, his eyes immediately drawn to the man
behind the large oak desk. Philip Grayson was in his late
fifties, with greying hair and piercing blue eyes that seemed
to assess Aidan in an instant.

'Mr Grayson, I'm DC Chilcott. Thank you for
agreeing to speak with me today.'

Grayson nodded curtly, gesturing to the chair across
from him. 'Let's get this over with, shall we? I have a
company to run.'

Aidan sat down, pulling out his notebook. 'I

understand, sir. I'll try to keep this brief. As you know, we're investigating the death of Emily Ashcroft. I was hoping you could tell me about her role here at EWMS.'

Grayson leaned back in his chair, his face a mask of practiced neutrality. 'Emily was a dedicated employee. She hadn't been with us long, but she'd impressed us all.'

'How long had EWMS employed her for?'

'Months, if that,' Grayson replied. 'She was fresh out of university, but she had good qualifications and knew her onions.'

Aidan nodded, making a note. 'I understand there was an incident between you and Emily shortly before her death. An argument, I believe?'

Grayson's eyes narrowed slightly. 'Who told you that?'

Aidan ignored the question, keeping his tone even. 'Can you tell me what the argument was about?'

There was a long pause as Grayson seemed to weigh his options. Finally, he sighed. 'It was a misunderstanding about some files Emily had accessed. Nothing more.'

'What kind of files?'

'I'm afraid that's confidential company information. You understand.'

Aidan felt a flicker of frustration but kept it from showing on his face. 'Mr Grayson, we're investigating a murder. Surely you can see how this information might be relevant?'

Grayson's jaw tightened. 'It really isn't. Emily accessed some information outside of her usual remit, which raised some security concerns. Audit trails showed some data had been printed out, but when we approached Emily she wasn't able to produce the print-outs, which led us to conclude she'd taken them off-site. We discussed it, and the matter was resolved.'

'Resolved how?' Aidan pressed.

'Emily explained she was working on an analysis for a potential new client. She'd been given verbal approval by her immediate supervisor but hadn't followed the proper documentation procedures. We clarified the protocols, and that was the end of it.'

Aidan made another note, his mind racing. Something didn't add up. 'And you're certain that was the end of it? No further issues?'

Grayson's eyes flashed with irritation. 'Are you implying something?'

'Not at all. I'm simply trying to build a complete picture of Emily's final days. If she'd only been with you a few months, you were free to let her go at any point. Especially if she'd flouted company protocols in that way.'

There was a tense silence. Aidan could almost see the gears turning in Grayson's head, calculating how much to reveal.

'Look,' Grayson finally said, leaning forward, 'I know how this might appear. But the truth is, Emily was a valued member of our team. Finding the right people in this industry isn't as easy as you might think. Her death is a tragedy, and we're all shocked by it. I can assure you it had nothing to do with her work here.'

Aidan raised an eyebrow. 'That's quite a strong assurance, Mr Grayson. What makes you so certain?'

Grayson's face flushed slightly. 'Because there's nothing in our line of work worth killing over. We're a legitimate business, operating well within environmental regulations.'

'I see,' Aidan said, making a mental note of Grayson's defensiveness. 'And everything has been above board? No issues with environmental compliance or waste management protocols?'

Grayson's eyes hardened. 'DC Chilcott, I've cooperated fully with your questions. But I won't sit here and have the integrity of my company questioned. If you have specific concerns about our operations, I suggest you take them up with our legal department.'

Aidan held up a placating hand. 'I'm not making any accusations, Mr Grayson. I'm simply following all possible leads in our investigation.'

'Well, I think we've covered everything relevant to your case,' Grayson said, standing up. 'If there's nothing else?'

Aidan stood as well, knowing he'd pushed as far as he could for now. 'Just one more thing, sir. Did Emily mention any concerns or fears in the days leading up to her death? Anything out of the ordinary?'

Grayson paused, a flicker of something – guilt? worry? – crossing his face. 'No, nothing I can recall. Emily was... she was fine. Professional as always.'

Aidan nodded, not entirely convinced. 'Thank you for your time, Mr Grayson. We'll be in touch if we have any further questions.'

As he left the office, Aidan's mind was whirling. Grayson's defensiveness pointed to something bigger. He needed to update Dexter and the team immediately. Whatever was going on at Environmental Waste Management Solutions, Aidan felt certain it was key to unravelling the mystery of Emily Ashcroft's death.

19

Dexter stormed into the office, the events of the previous evening still churning in his gut. He'd barely slept, his mind racing with thoughts of Elijah's smug face and pointed accusations. Enough was enough.

The early morning light filtered through the blinds, casting long shadows across the empty desks. Dexter glanced at his watch. 7:30 AM. He'd come in early, hoping to gather his thoughts before the day properly began.

He tossed his bag onto his desk with more force than necessary, the thud echoing in the quiet room. Sara, already at her desk, looked up from her computer, startled by the sudden noise.

'Morning,' she said, her tone cautious. 'You're in early. Everything alright?'

Dexter ran a hand over his shaved head, feeling the familiar stubble beneath his palm. He exhaled heavily, the weight of the past twenty-four hours pressing down on him. 'No,' he admitted. 'Not really.'

Sara's brow furrowed, concern etching itself across her features. 'Want to talk about it?'

For a moment, Dexter hesitated. He glanced around the office, double-checking that they were indeed alone. The rest of the team wouldn't be in for at least another half hour. Elijah's desk, directly across from his own, stood empty - a sight that brought both relief and a renewed surge of anger.

Making a decision, he perched on the edge of Sara's desk, leaning in close to keep his voice low. 'It's Elijah,' he said, the name coming out like a curse. 'He's up to something.'

Sara's eyes widened slightly, her fingers stilling on her keyboard. 'What do you mean?'

'He confronted me last night in the car park. Brought up the Fletcher incident.'

'Oh,' Sara said, her voice barely above a whisper. 'That must have been uncomfortable.'

Dexter nodded, oblivious to the slight tremor in Sara's voice. 'It was. But that's not the point. How did he even know about it? He's only been here five minutes.'

Sara shrugged, her eyes darting away from Dexter's intense gaze. 'Maybe someone mentioned it in passing?'

'Maybe,' Dexter said, his tone unconvinced. He stood up, pacing in front of Sara's desk. 'But it felt... targeted. Like he was trying to get under my skin.'

'I'm sure it wasn't—'

'No,' Dexter interrupted, stopping his pacing to face Sara. 'There's more to this. He's been undermining me, going behind my back to reporters. And now this? It's not a coincidence.'

Sara swallowed hard, her hands fidgeting with a pen on her desk. 'What are you going to do?'

Dexter's jaw set, determination flashing in his eyes. 'I'm going to unmask him. Find out what he's really up to, who he's been talking to. I won't let him jeopardise this team or our work.'

As he spoke, Dexter failed to notice Sara's face paling slightly, her fingers tensing around the pen.

'Are you sure that's wise?' she asked, her voice strained. 'Maybe you should talk to Caroline first?'

Dexter shook his head, resuming his pacing. 'No, I need to handle this myself. I can't have the boss thinking I can't manage my own team.'

He turned back to his desk, missing the flash of panic that crossed Sara's face.

'Just... be careful, yeah?' Sara said, her voice barely steady. 'We don't want to create unnecessary tension in the team.'

Dexter nodded absently, already lost in thought about how to proceed. 'Don't worry. I'll be discreet. But I'm going to get to the bottom of this, one way or another.'

He sat down at his desk and booted up his computer, the familiar hum filling the quiet office. As he waited for the system to load, Dexter's mind raced with possibilities. Could Elijah have other connections within the force? Was someone feeding him information? Or was this all part of some larger plan?

'Do you think...' Sara began, then hesitated. Dexter looked up, raising an eyebrow. 'Do you think maybe you're reading too much into this? Elijah's new, after all. Maybe he's just trying to fit in, prove himself.'

Dexter leaned back in his chair, considering Sara's words. 'You didn't see him last night, Sara. The way he spoke, the look in his eyes. This isn't about fitting in. It's about undermining me, maybe even taking my place.'

Sara's eyes widened. 'Surely not. He's only just joined the team.'

'Exactly,' Dexter said, leaning forward. 'Which makes me wonder who he's really working for. This feels bigger than just office politics.'

He stood up again, unable to sit still with the energy thrumming through him. 'I need to find out who he's been talking to. Someone must be feeding him information.'

Sara's hand tightened around her pen. 'How do you plan to do that?'

Dexter's eyes narrowed, a plan already forming in his mind. 'I'm going to start by checking his comms. See who he's been talking to, both inside and outside the force.'

'Dexter, you can't do that,' Sara said, her voice firm despite her unease. 'That's not just unethical, it's illegal. We'd need a formal investigation from Internal Affairs for anything like that.'

Dexter paused, taken aback by Sara's directness. He

knew she was right, but the frustration and anger clouding his judgment made it hard to admit.

'You're right,' he conceded after a moment. 'I'm just... I feel like I'm being backed into a corner here.'

Sara's expression softened slightly. 'I understand you're frustrated, but we have to do this by the book. If you really think there's something going on, you need to talk to Caroline.'

Dexter nodded, though reluctantly. 'Yeah, I know. I just hate the thought of not being able to handle this myself.'

'It's not about handling it yourself,' Sara said. 'It's about doing what's right for the team and the investigation.'

As Dexter turned back to his computer, he remained blissfully unaware of Sara's inner turmoil. He didn't see her hand trembling as she reached for her mobile phone, or the way her eyes darted nervously towards the door.

All Dexter knew was that he had a mission now. Elijah thought he could play games? Well, two could play at that. And Dexter was determined to come out on top, no matter what it took.

The sound of voices in the corridor signalled the arrival of the rest of the team. Dexter straightened in his chair, composing his features into a mask of calm professionalism. As Elijah walked in, Dexter met his gaze coolly, refusing to show any sign of the turmoil within.

The game was on, and Dexter was playing for keeps.

20

The warm glow of The Wheatsheaf's vintage lamps cast long shadows across the worn oak tables as Caroline led her team into their usual corner. The familiar scent of hops and polish hung in the air, a comforting constant amidst the turmoil of recent weeks. She'd suggested this impromptu drink with a forced casualness that fooled no one, her eyes darting between Dexter and Elijah as she'd made the proposal back at the station.

Now, settled into the bench with a gin and tonic condensing before her, Caroline surveyed her team. The weight of unspoken tensions seemed to press down on them all, muffling even the usual buzz of after-work chatter that filled the pub.

Dexter's fingers curled around his pint glass, his knuckles white with tension. He was acutely aware of Elijah's presence across the table, the other man's easy smile a stark contrast to the knot in Dexter's stomach. Sara sat beside Elijah, her posture rigid, eyes flicking between the two men as if waiting for a spark to ignite.

Aidan, ever the peacemaker, cleared his throat. 'So,' he began, his voice a touch too bright, 'any thoughts on Op Helix? I can't help feeling we're missing something obvious.'

A beat of silence followed, heavy with unspoken words. Caroline opened her mouth to respond, but Elijah beat her to it.

'Actually,' he said, setting down his glass with a soft clink, 'before we dive back into work talk, there's something I'd like to say.' He turned to face Dexter directly, his expression open and earnest. 'Dex, I know things have been... strained between us lately. I think it's time we buried the hatchet.'

The pub's background chatter seemed to fade away as all eyes turned to Dexter. He felt the weight of their gazes, especially Caroline's, boring into him. The moment stretched, taut as a wire.

'What, in the back of my head?' The words escaped before Dexter could stop them, his tone sharper than he'd intended. As soon as they left his mouth, he regretted them.

A collective intake of breath followed. Sara's eyes widened, while Aidan looked down at his drink, suddenly fascinated by the condensation on his glass. Caroline's lips tightened into a thin line, disappointment etched in the furrow of her brow.

Elijah, however, merely chuckled, raising his hands in

a placating gesture. 'I suppose I deserved that. Look, I know I haven't made the best impression since joining the team. But I genuinely want us to move past this. What do you say, Dex? Clean slate?'

Dexter hesitated, his instincts screaming at him not to trust Elijah's sudden olive branch. But as he glanced around at his colleagues, he realised he had no choice. Refusing would only make him look petty and unreasonable. He could almost hear the thoughts running through their minds - why couldn't he just let it go?

'Sure,' Dexter said finally, forcing a smile that felt more like a grimace. 'Clean slate.'

Elijah beamed, raising his glass. 'To new beginnings, eh?'

The others joined in the toast, a palpable sense of relief washing over the group. As conversation slowly resumed, Dexter couldn't shake the feeling that he'd just been outmanoeuvred. He took a long swig of his beer, the bitter taste matching his mood.

Caroline leaned in close, her voice low enough that only he could hear. 'That was the right move, Dex. I know it's not easy, but we need this team pulling together.'

Dexter nodded, not trusting himself to speak. Across the table, he caught Elijah's eye. The other man raised his glass in a silent salute, a gesture that could have been friendly or mocking. Dexter couldn't quite tell, and that uncertainty gnawed at him.

As the evening wore on, Dexter found himself participating more in the conversation, almost against his will. Elijah, for his part, was the picture of affability, cracking jokes and sharing anecdotes that had even Aidan chuckling. Sara seemed to relax as well, her earlier tension melting away as she laughed at one of Elijah's stories.

'You should have seen the look on the guy's face,' Elijah was saying, gesturing with his half-empty glass. 'There he was, thinking he'd got away with it, and then boom – we pull out the CCTV footage he didn't know existed.'

'Classic,' Aidan chuckled. 'Bet he sang like a canary after that.'

'Oh, you have no idea,' Elijah grinned. 'Started confessing to things we hadn't even accused him of yet.'

The laughter that followed felt genuine, and Dexter found himself smiling despite his reservations. He had to admit, Elijah could spin a good yarn when he wanted to.

As the night progressed, the conversation drifted from work anecdotes to more personal topics. Aidan regaled them with tales of his latest DIY disaster, while Sara shared stories from her recent weekend hike in the Peak District. Even Caroline loosened up, sharing a funny story about Archie's first attempts at baking.

Dexter contributed where he could, but he couldn't shake the feeling of being an outsider looking in. Every time Elijah spoke, Dexter found himself analysing the words, searching for hidden meanings or veiled insults. It was exhausting.

'Another round?' Elijah offered as he drained the last of his pint.

There was a chorus of agreement, and Elijah stood to head to the bar. To Dexter's surprise, Elijah turned to him. 'Give us a hand, Dex?'

Caught off guard, Dexter nodded and followed Elijah to the bar. As they waited for the bartender, Elijah turned to him, his expression serious.

'Listen, Dex,' he said, his voice low and earnest. 'I meant what I said earlier. I know things got off on the wrong foot between us, but I really do want to make this work. We're on the same team, after all.'

Dexter studied Elijah's face, searching for any sign of insincerity. 'Why the sudden change of heart?'

Elijah sighed, running a hand through his hair. 'Look, I know I can come across as a bit... intense sometimes. Truth is, I was nervous about fitting in here. The culture at EMSOU was totally different, and I think I misjudged how to interact with you all. I'm not making excuses, mind. Just trying to explain.'

There was a vulnerability in Elijah's admission that caught Dexter off guard. Could he have misjudged the man?

'How about we grab a proper drink sometime, just the two of us?' Elijah suggested. 'Clear the air properly, without an audience.'

Dexter hesitated, then nodded. 'Sure, why not?'

As they carried the drinks back to the table, Dexter felt a mix of emotions he couldn't quite untangle. Part of him wanted to believe in Elijah's sincerity, to accept this olive branch at face value. But another part, the detective in him perhaps, couldn't help but remain wary.

The rest of the evening passed in a blur of conversation and laughter. By the time they were ready to leave, the atmosphere had lightened considerably. As they gathered their coats, Dexter caught Caroline's eye. She gave him an approving nod, and he felt a twinge of something - relief? guilt? - in his chest.

Outside, the cool Rutland night air was a refreshing change from the pub's warmth. As the team said their goodbyes, Dexter found himself standing next to Elijah once more.

'Thanks for hearing me out, Dex,' Elijah said, clapping him on the shoulder. 'I'm looking forward to that drink.'

Dexter nodded, managing a small smile. 'Yeah, me too.'

As he watched Elijah walk away, chatting animatedly with Sara, Dexter felt a complex mix of emotions. Had he just made a breakthrough in a difficult working relationship? Or had he let his guard down at precisely the wrong moment?

The question lingered in his mind as he bid goodnight to the others and began the walk back to his car. The streets of Oakham were quietening down, with most shops already closed for the night. The crisp evening air carried the scent of freshly cut grass from nearby Cutts Close park.

As if on cue, the bells of All Saints Church began to toll, the sound reverberating loudly through the town centre. Dexter glanced at his watch - ten o'clock already. The drive back to Leicester loomed ahead, giving him ample time to mull over the evening's events.

His footsteps echoed on the pavement as he walked, his mind replaying the conversation with Elijah. He thought about the man's apparent sincerity, Caroline's approval, the team's relief at the easing of tensions. It all seemed too neat, too perfect.

But then again, wasn't that what he'd wanted? For the team to work together smoothly, without the undercurrent of hostility that had been plaguing them?

As he reached his car, Dexter realised he'd have to make a choice. He could continue to second-guess every interaction, to look for hidden motives in every gesture. Or he could choose to take Elijah at his word, to give this fresh start a genuine chance.

Either way, he knew one thing for certain: the dynamics of their team had shifted tonight. What that would mean for their work, for Operation Helix, for all of them – only time would tell.

Dexter unlocked his car and slid into the driver's seat, leaving the questions of the night behind in Oakham. As he started the engine and began his journey home, he knew that tomorrow would bring new challenges, new leads to follow. For now, he needed to focus on the road ahead.

21

Caroline's car pulled up outside Sophie Trent's modest terraced house. The late afternoon sun cast long shadows across the quiet street, giving an air of tranquility that belied the gravity of their visit. She glanced at Aidan in the passenger seat, noting the determined set of his jaw.

'Ready?' she asked, her hand on the door handle.

Aidan nodded, his eyes fixed on Sophie's front door. 'Let's do this.'

As they approached the house, Caroline couldn't shake the feeling that they were on the verge of a breakthrough. The pieces of the puzzle were starting to fall into place, but the picture they formed was far more sinister than she had initially imagined.

Caroline rapped sharply on the door. A moment passed before they heard movement inside, and then the door swung open to reveal Sophie. Her eyes were red-rimmed, and she looked pale and drawn.

'Detective Inspector Hills,' Sophie said, her voice barely above a whisper. 'And... Detective Constable Chilcott, right?'

Aidan nodded, offering a small, reassuring smile.

'May we come in, Sophie?' Caroline asked gently. 'We have some questions about Emily's work at EWMS.'

Sophie's eyes widened slightly, a flicker of fear crossing her face before she quickly masked it. She stepped back, wordlessly inviting them inside.

The living room was neat but lived-in, with stacks of environmental science textbooks and journals scattered across the coffee table. Sophie perched on the edge of an armchair, her hands clasped tightly in her lap.

'Sophie,' Caroline began, her tone gentle but firm, 'we've been looking into Emily's work at EWMS. We believe she may have uncovered something... concerning.'

Sophie's breath hitched, her knuckles whitening as she gripped her hands tighter. 'I... I don't know what you mean,' she stammered, her eyes darting between Caroline and Aidan.

Aidan leaned forward slightly. 'Sophie, we know you and Emily were friends. We also know you both studied Environmental Science. If Emily was going to speak to anyone about work concerns, it would have been you.'

A tear slipped down Sophie's cheek. She brushed it away quickly, taking a shaky breath. 'You don't understand,' she whispered. 'It's bigger than you think. Dangerous.'

Caroline's pulse quickened. They were close to a

breakthrough; she could feel it. 'Sophie, we can protect you. But we need to know what Emily found out. What's the company hiding?'

Sophie stood abruptly, moving to the window. She stared out at the street, her arms wrapped tightly around herself. For a long moment, the only sound in the room was her ragged breathing.

Finally, she turned back to face them, her eyes brimming with tears and something else – determination. 'They're dumping waste,' she said, her voice barely audible. 'Illegally. Into the rivers that feed Rutland Water.'

Caroline and Aidan exchanged a glance, the implications of this revelation sinking in.

'Which rivers?' Aidan asked, his pen poised over his notebook.

'The Nene and the Welland,' Sophie replied, her voice stronger now. 'Emily... she found discrepancies in the water quality reports. At first, she thought it was just a mistake in the data. But then she started digging deeper.'

Caroline leaned forward, her voice urgent. 'What did she find, Sophie?'

Sophie's face crumpled. 'It's not just regular waste. It's... it's toxic. Industrial chemicals, sewage... things that should never, ever be in our water supply. And it's been going on for years.'

'Jesus,' Aidan muttered, scribbling furiously in his notebook.

'The water company clean it all up, obviously, so it's all within safe levels by the time it reaches the taps, but that's not the point. EWMS are deliberately flouting regulations on the safe disposal of toxic waste. The rules are really clear.'

'Why didn't Emily come to us?' Caroline asked, struggling to keep her voice level as the magnitude of the situation became clear.

Sophie laughed bitterly. 'She tried. She went to her superiors first, thinking they'd want to fix it. But they shut her down. Told her she was mistaken, that she'd misinterpreted the data. When she pushed back, they threatened her.'

'Threatened her how?' Caroline pressed.

'They said they'd ruin her career. That no one would believe her over a respected company like EWMS.' Sophie's voice broke. 'She was scared, but she wouldn't let it go. She was gathering more evidence, building a stronger case. She wanted to blow the whistle, but she needed to be sure.'

Caroline felt a chill run down her spine. 'And you think this is why she was killed?'

Sophie nodded, fresh tears spilling down her cheeks. 'It has to be. She was getting close to exposing them. And there's so much money involved, so many powerful people who'd do anything to keep this quiet.'

Aidan looked up from his notebook, his face grim. 'Sophie, do you have any of the evidence Emily collected? Anything at all?'

Sophie hesitated, then walked over to a wooden side unit. She opened a drawer and took out a USB drive.

'Emily gave me this,' she said, holding it out with a trembling hand. 'For safekeeping. She said if anything happened to her, I should take it to the authorities. But after she died... I was too scared. I thought they might come for me next.'

Caroline took the USB drive, feeling the implicit weight of its contents. 'You've done the right thing, Sophie. We'll protect you. But we need to know everything you know about this.'

Sophie nodded, sinking back into her chair. As she began to speak, detailing what Emily had discovered about the illegal dumping of waste, Caroline felt a mix of emotions wash over her. Horror at the scale of the environmental crime. Anger at the corruption that had allowed it to continue. And a grim determination to bring those responsible to justice.

As Sophie's story unfolded, Caroline caught Aidan's eye. They both knew that this case had just become much bigger and more dangerous than they had ever anticipated. But they also knew that they couldn't back down now. For Emily's sake, for Sophie's, and for the countless people whose health had been put at risk, they had to see this through to the end.

22

The clink of glasses and bursts of laughter spilled out onto the street as Dexter approached the Three Crowns in Wymeswold.

Dexter paused at the entrance, his hand hovering over it. He'd driven nearly half an hour for this drink with Elijah, and now that he was here, a knot of uncertainty tightened in his stomach. Taking a deep breath, he pushed the door open and stepped inside.

Dexter's eyes scanned the room, finally landing on Elijah. He sat at a table near the back, still clad in his cricket whites, a half-empty pint glass in front of him. His cricket bag leaned against the wall, as if standing guard.

As Dexter threaded his way through the tables, he felt the curious gazes of the locals. In a village this size, a new face never went unnoticed.

'Dexter!' Elijah called out, raising his glass in greeting. 'Glad you could make it. What's your poison?'

'It's alright, I'll get them,' Dexter replied. 'Pint of bitter, please,' he told the bartender, a grey-haired man with a face that spoke of years spent in this very pub.

Drink in hand, Dexter joined Elijah at the table. Despite the easing of tensions over the past week, he couldn't quite shake the wariness that had taken root in him.

'Cheers,' Elijah said, clinking his glass against Dexter's. 'Thanks for coming out this way. Thought it'd be easier to meet here after the match.'

Dexter nodded, taking a sip of his beer. 'No worries. How'd it go?'

Elijah's face lit up. 'Not bad, actually. We managed to scrape a win.'

'Yeah? Who were you playing?'

'None other than the mighty Coddington and Winthorpe Development XI.'

Dexter raised an eyebrow. 'Blimey. One for the history books.'

'Tell me about it,' Elijah chuckled. 'We spent half the match just trying to fit their name on the scoreboard. We abbreviated it to "C&W Dev XI" in the end.'

Dexter found himself smiling despite his reservations. 'So, you're playing for the seconds?'

'Yeah, work makes it hard to commit to the firsts. Can't exactly tell a murderer to hold off because I've got a cricket match, can I?'

They shared a laugh at that, the ice between them beginning to thaw.

'You follow cricket much?' Elijah asked, leaning back in his chair.

Dexter nodded. 'Big Leicestershire supporter. Been going to Grace Road since I was a kid.'

'Ah, a true fan then. Sticking with them through thick and thin.'

'Mostly thin these days,' Dexter admitted with a rueful smile.

'Speaking of which,' Elijah said, reaching for his bag, 'what do you think of this beauty?' He pulled out a gleaming cricket bat, its wood polished to a rich honey colour.

Dexter leaned forward, his interest piqued despite himself. 'That's a nice piece of willow.'

'Latest model from Gray-Nicolls,' Elijah said proudly. 'Feel the weight of it.'

Before Dexter could respond, Elijah was already passing the bat across the table. Dexter took it, feeling the comfortable weight in his hands. He turned it over, admiring the grains of the wood and the precise placement of the maker's label.

'Good balance,' Dexter commented, giving the bat a gentle swing. 'No wonder you're hitting sixes with this.'

Elijah beamed. 'It's treated me well so far. Here, have a proper swing.'

Dexter stood up, gripping the bat properly. He took a careful practice swing, mindful of the other patrons. 'Yeah, that's a great bat. Thanks for letting me have a go.'

He handed the bat back to Elijah, who returned it to his bag with an almost reverent care.

The conversation flowed more easily after that, moving from cricket to work, family, and back to cricket again. Dexter found himself relaxing, the beer and easy banter working their magic.

'So there I am,' Elijah was saying, gesturing with his nearly empty glass, 'facing their fastest bowler. This lad's built like a brick shithouse, and he's steaming in like he's got a personal vendetta against me.'

Dexter leaned in, caught up in the story despite himself.

'Ball comes down, an absolute corker of a delivery. I swing, connect, and next thing I know, the ball's sailing over the boundary.'

'Six?'

'Six,' Elijah confirmed with a grin. 'Should've seen the look on his face. Think I might have ruined his weekend.'

Dexter chuckled, draining the last of his pint. 'Sounds like quite a match.'

'It was,' Elijah nodded, then glanced at his watch. 'Christ, is that the time already? Suppose I should think about heading off.'

Dexter felt a flicker of his earlier wariness return. 'Yeah, probably should. Got to drive back to Leicester.'

'Right, of course,' Elijah said. 'Think I'll finish this one off first, then walk home. I'm only down the road. Listen, Dex,' he added as Dexter stood to leave, 'I'm glad we did this. Feels good to clear the air, you know?'

Dexter nodded, not quite meeting Elijah's eyes. 'Yeah, it's been... good.'

'We should do it again sometime. Maybe catch a Leicestershire match together?'

'Maybe,' Dexter said noncommittally. 'Anyway, I'd better get going. Thanks for the invite.'

'No worries, mate. Drive safe,' Elijah said, clapping Dexter on the shoulder.

Dexter nodded and headed out to the car park. The cool night air was a refreshing change from the stuffy warmth of the pub. As he walked to his car, he found himself mulling over the evening. It had gone better than he'd expected, but he still couldn't shake a lingering sense of unease.

He got into his car and started the engine, watching in the rearview mirror as Elijah emerged from the pub, cricket bag slung over his shoulder. Elijah gave a small wave, which Dexter returned before pulling out of the car park.

As he drove back towards Leicester, Dexter's mind wandered to the case waiting for him back in Oakham. Operation Helix was far from over, and he needed to focus on that, not on trying to decipher Elijah's every move.

The roads were quiet, giving Dexter plenty of time to think. By the time he reached his flat, he'd almost convinced himself that his suspicions about Elijah were unfounded. Maybe, just maybe, they could work together after all.

23

Elijah watched Dexter's taillights disappear down the road, then turned towards the car park. He'd nursed his single pint all evening, mindful of the drive home. The Three Crowns was a bit of a trek from where he lived, but tonight's meeting had been necessary.

A twig crunched under his feet as he crossed the nearly empty car park. Most of the other patrons had already left or gone inside, leaving the area quiet save for the distant hum of traffic. Elijah's hand tightened on the strap of his cricket bag as he approached his car.

He paused, keys in hand, and glanced at his watch. Ten o'clock.

A rustle of movement caught his attention. Elijah turned, his posture tense. A hooded figure stepped out from behind a nearby vehicle.

The figure said nothing, advancing silently.

Elijah took a step back, his legs touching his car. His grip on the cricket bag loosened.

The attacker lunged forward, tearing the bag from Elijah's shoulder. There was a brief struggle, Elijah's protests cut short as the first blow landed.

A series of dull thuds followed, each impact driving the air from Elijah's lungs. He fell to his knees, then onto his side, curling into himself as the assault continued. The cold ground of the car park pressed against his cheek, his world narrowing to the rhythm of pain and the sound of his own ragged breathing.

Finally, mercifully, it stopped. As footsteps retreated into the night, Elijah lay still, his cricket bat discarded nearby, a silent witness to the violence that had just occurred.

24

Caroline couldn't remember the last time she'd worn heels. The gentle click as she walked across the polished floor of The Noel in Whitwell felt alien, almost silly. But then, everything about tonight felt a bit surreal.

It had been Mark's idea, of course. A proper night out, he'd said. No work talk, no kid talk. Just the two of them, a nice meal, and a few drinks. Caroline had to admit, it felt good to let her hair down a bit.

'Sorry about that. Shouldn't have downed that pint of water before we left. Anyway. This is nice,' she said, smiling at Mark across the table. 'We should do this more often.'

Mark grinned, raising his glass of red wine. 'Told you. Although I'm not sure the bank balance could handle it if we did.'

'To us,' Caroline said, clinking her glass against his.

'And to finally managing a night out without a crisis at work or with the kids.'

'Don't jinx it,' Mark laughed, taking a sip of his wine.

The conversation flowed easily as they worked their way through their starters. Caroline found herself genuinely relaxing, the constant hum of work and family responsibilities fading into the background.

'So,' Mark said, as the waiter cleared their plates, 'I've been thinking.'

'Dangerous, that.'

'Ha bloody ha. No, seriously. I've been thinking about that cycling holiday we talked about. What do you reckon? Think we could manage a week in the Peak District next summer?'

Caroline raised an eyebrow. 'With the boys? You think Josh and Archie are ready for that much cycling?'

'They're not babies anymore, love. Josh is fourteen now, and Archie's ten. It'd do them good to get away from their screens for a bit.'

'True,' Caroline mused. 'And I suppose it would be nice to have a proper family holiday.'

Their main courses arrived, momentarily halting the conversation. Caroline cut into her steak, savouring the first bite. It was perfectly cooked, just how she liked it.

'This is good,' she said. 'Although I'm not sure I'll be able to finish it all.'

Mark grinned. 'I'm sure I can help you out there.'

They chatted and laughed their way through the rest of the meal, trading stories about work and the boys.

Caroline found herself remembering why she'd fallen in love with Mark in the first place. His easy smile, his quick wit, the way he could make her laugh even on her worst days.

'You know,' she said, pushing her half-finished plate away, 'I was a bit skeptical about moving here at first. But I think it's the best decision we ever made.'

Mark reached across the table and squeezed her hand. 'Me too. It's been good for all of us, I reckon. The boys seem happier, and you... well, you're not as stressed as you used to be in London.'

Caroline nodded. 'It's different here. Slower. I mean, don't get me wrong, the job's still challenging, but it's not the same constant pressure cooker it was in the Met.'

'And the neighbours are friendlier,' Mark added with a wink.

'God, yes. Remember Mrs. Calderwood and her yappy little dog?'

They both laughed at the memory of their former neighbour and her incessantly barking Chihuahua.

'Although,' Caroline said, 'I do sometimes miss the excitement of the Met. Is that awful of me?'

'Awful? No, not at all. Wrong, is what it is. You've had more than enough excitement since you've been here. So much for a quiet life in the country.'

Caroline lowered her head slightly. 'Sorry. Sometimes I wonder if I unintentionally create all this drama or whether it just follows me around everywhere.'

Mark shook his head. 'Nah. You're just the right

person for the job at the right time, that's all. It's part of who you are. You're good at what you do, and it's natural to want to use those skills.'

'Maybe,' Caroline mused. 'But I wouldn't trade this for anything. The quiet evenings, the weekends with the boys. It's... it's home, you know?'

Mark smiled softly. 'I know exactly what you mean.'

They lapsed into a comfortable silence as the waiter cleared their plates and handed them the dessert menus.

'Fancy sharing a chocolate fondant?' Mark asked, eyeing the menu.

Caroline patted her stomach. 'God, I shouldn't. But go on then, twist my arm.'

As they waited for their dessert, they people-watched, making up stories about the other diners. The Noel was busy, filled with the gentle hum of conversation and the clink of cutlery on plates.

Their dessert arrived, two spoons nestled alongside the perfectly formed chocolate pudding. As Caroline dug her spoon in, releasing a flow of molten chocolate, her phone buzzed in her clutch bag.

She fished it out, frowning at the screen. 'It's Tom,' she said, a note of concern creeping into her voice.

'Babysitter Tom? Why would he be calling?'

Caroline answered the call, her relaxed mood evaporating as she listened to Tom's panicked voice. 'We're on our way,' she said, her tone clipped and professional. 'Tell them we won't be long.'

She ended the call and turned to Mark, her eyes wide

with fear. 'It's Archie. He's collapsed. Tom's called an ambulance.'

Mark's face paled. 'What? What's happened? He was fine when we left.'

'I know,' Caroline said, already gathering her things. 'We need to go. Now.'

As they hurried out of the restaurant, their perfect evening shattered, Caroline found herself wishing, not for the first time, that she believed in God. Because right now, she'd give anything for someone to pray to.

25

The harsh fluorescent lights of the hospital corridor seemed to buzz in Caroline's ears as she sat rigidly in the uncomfortable plastic chair. Her eyes were fixed on Archie's small form in the hospital bed, watching the steady rise and fall of his chest. Mark sat beside her, his head in his hands.

It had been four hours since they'd rushed from The Noel, their perfect evening shattered by a panicked phone call. Four hours of tests, questions, and gut-wrenching worry.

A nurse entered the room, checking Archie's vitals and the IV drip in his arm. Caroline watched her every move, her detective's instincts kicking in, searching for any sign, any clue as to what was wrong with her son.

'How's he doing?' she asked, her voice sounding strange to her own ears.

The nurse smiled reassuringly. 'He's stable. The doctor will be in shortly to discuss the test results with you.'

As if on cue, a tall woman entered the room, a tablet in her hand. 'Mr and Mrs Hills? My name's Priya Sharma. I'm a consultant neurologist,' she added, her voice calm and reassuring.

Caroline stood up, extending her hand. 'Detective Inspector Hills,' she said automatically, then caught herself. 'I mean, Caroline. This is my husband, Mark.'

The consultant shook both their hands. 'I understand this must be a frightening time for you. I'd like to go over what we know so far and discuss our next steps.'

Mark looked up, his face pale. 'Is he going to be okay?'

'Archie is stable now,' the consultant assured them. 'What he experienced was a tonic-clonic seizure, formerly known as a grand mal seizure. It's alarming to witness, but it doesn't necessarily indicate a serious underlying condition.'

Caroline nodded, her mind racing. 'But it could be epilepsy, couldn't it?'

The consultant eyebrows rose slightly. 'It's a possibility we're considering. May I ask why you specifically mentioned epilepsy?'

'My father had it,' Mark said quietly. 'And my uncle.'

'I see,' the consultant said, making a note on her tablet. 'That family history is certainly relevant. However, it's important to understand that a single seizure doesn't necessarily mean epilepsy. We typically wait for a second unprovoked seizure before making that diagnosis.'

Caroline leaned forward. 'What about his test results? The blood tests, the... the brain scan thing?'

'The EEG,' Sharma answered. 'Well, Archie's blood work came back normal, which is good. It rules out some potential causes like electrolyte imbalances or infections. The CT scan didn't show any structural abnormalities in his brain, which is also positive.'

'But?' Caroline pressed, sensing there was more.

Sharma nodded. 'The EEG did show some irregular brain wave patterns. This doesn't definitively diagnose epilepsy, but it does suggest an increased likelihood of future seizures.'

Mark took Caroline's hand, squeezing it tightly. 'So what happens now?'

'We'd like to keep Archie overnight for observation,' the consultant explained. 'We'll continue to monitor his brain activity. In the morning, we'll do a more comprehensive EEG.'

Caroline nodded, her detective mind kicking into high gear. 'What should we be looking out for when he comes home? Are there... signs we might have missed?'

The consultant looked thoughtful. 'It's common for parents to recall certain behaviours in hindsight. Have you noticed Archie having brief staring spells? Moments where he seems to "zone out" for a few seconds?'

Caroline and Mark exchanged a glance. 'He does that sometimes when he's playing video games,' Mark said slowly. 'We thought he was just really focused.'

'Any unexplained falls? Periods of confusion?' Sharma prompted.

Caroline felt a chill run down her spine. 'He's always been a bit clumsy. Trips over his own feet sometimes.'

Sharma nodded. 'These could potentially be absence seizures or focal seizures. They're much subtler than what you witnessed tonight, which is why they often go unnoticed.'

'Christ,' Mark muttered. 'How did we miss this?'

'You haven't missed anything,' the consultant said firmly. 'These symptoms can be easy to overlook, especially in active children. The important thing is that we're investigating now.'

Caroline took a deep breath, forcing herself to focus. 'What's the treatment plan? Assuming it is epilepsy.'

'If Archie is diagnosed with epilepsy, there are several effective medications we can use to control seizures,' Sharma explained. 'We'd start with a low dose and adjust as needed. Many people with epilepsy lead completely normal lives with proper management.'

Mark nodded, but Caroline could see the worry etched on his face. She squeezed his hand, trying to offer comfort even as her own mind raced with questions and concerns.

'Will he need to stop playing sports?' Mark asked. 'He loves football.'

Priya Sharma shook her head. 'Not necessarily. We'd need to take precautions, but physical activity is generally encouraged. It's about finding the right balance.'

Caroline's eyes drifted back to Archie. He looked so

small in the hospital bed, so vulnerable. It was hard to reconcile this image with the boisterous ten-year-old who'd been pestering them for a new bike just yesterday.

'When will he wake up?' she asked, her voice barely above a whisper.

'Soon,' Sharma assured her. 'It's perfectly normal for the post-ictal phase – that's the recovery period after a seizure – to last anywhere from a few minutes to a few hours. Archie's been sleeping peacefully, which is good. His body needs the rest.'

As if on cue, Archie stirred slightly, his eyelids fluttering. Caroline and Mark were instantly on their feet, moving to either side of the bed.

'Archie?' Caroline called softly, brushing his hair back from his forehead. 'Can you hear me, sweetheart?'

Archie's eyes opened slowly, confusion evident in his gaze. 'Mum?' he mumbled. 'Where am I?'

'You're in the hospital, mate,' Mark said, his voice thick with emotion. 'You gave us a bit of a scare.'

The consultant stepped forward, shining a small light in Archie's eyes. 'Hello, Archie. I'm one of the doctors here. How are you feeling?'

'Tired,' Archie said, his voice small. 'My head hurts.'

'That's normal,' the consultant assured him. 'You've had a big night. Do you remember what happened?'

Archie's brow furrowed. 'I was... playing on my tablet. Then everything went weird. Lights and colours. Then nothing.'

Caroline and Mark exchanged a worried glance over Archie's head. Sharma made a note on her tablet.

'That's okay, Archie,' she said kindly. 'You're doing great. We're going to do some more tests later in the day, but for now, you should rest.'

As Sharma stepped back, Caroline leaned in, pressing a kiss to Archie's forehead. 'We're right here, love. Try to get some sleep.'

Archie nodded, his eyes already drifting closed again. Within moments, his breathing had evened out into sleep.

Caroline straightened up, meeting Mark's worried gaze. She could see her own fears reflected in his eyes – fear of the unknown, fear for their son's future. But beneath that, she saw determination, love, and a stubborn refusal to be beaten.

Whatever this was – epilepsy or something else – they would face it together. As a family.

Priya Sharma cleared her throat softly. 'I'll leave you with Archie now. The nurse will be checking in regularly, and I'll be back in the morning to discuss the next steps.'

As the doctor left, Caroline sank back into her chair, suddenly exhausted. Mark sat beside her, wrapping an arm around her shoulders.

'He'll be okay,' Mark murmured, though Caroline wasn't sure if he was reassuring her or himself. 'We'll get through this.'

Caroline nodded, leaning into his embrace. As she watched Archie sleep, his chest rising and falling steadily, she made a silent vow. Whatever it took, whatever they had to face, she would protect her son. It was a mystery she was determined to solve, a case where failure was not an option.

Because this wasn't just another investigation. This was Archie. This was family. And for Caroline, nothing in the world mattered more than that.

The room fell quiet, save for the steady beep of the heart monitor and the distant sounds of the hospital beyond. Caroline found herself counting Archie's breaths, each one a reminder that he was here, he was alive, he was fighting.

Mark's hand found hers again, their fingers intertwining. In that moment, surrounded by the sterile white of the hospital room, Caroline felt a surge of gratitude for her husband's steady presence. They'd faced challenges before, but nothing quite like this.

As the night wore on, nurses came and went, checking vitals and adjusting equipment. Caroline and Mark took turns dozing in the uncomfortable chairs, neither willing to leave Archie's side for more than a moment.

In the quiet hours before dawn, Caroline found herself reflecting on the evening that now felt a lifetime ago. The laughter, the wine, the plans for a cycling holiday – all swept away in an instant. Life, she mused, had a way of reminding you what really mattered.

Caroline straightened in her chair, ready to face whatever the new day might bring. There would be more tests, more questions, more worries. But they would face them together, as a family.

And no matter what happened, Caroline knew one thing for certain: nothing would ever be the same again.

26

The stale scent of yesterday's coffee mingled with the sharp tang of disinfectant as Caroline pushed open the door of Oakham police station. Another Monday, another chance to unravel the knot that was Operation Helix. The weekend had brought no breakthrough in Operation Helix, and she could feel the pressure mounting with each passing day.

As she approached the CID office, she noticed a small commotion near the entrance. Officers were gathered around someone, their voices a mix of concern and curiosity. Caroline quickened her pace, a sense of unease settling in her stomach.

The crowd parted as she neared, revealing Elijah standing in the centre. Caroline's breath caught in her throat. Elijah's face was a map of bruises, his left eye swollen nearly shut, and a nasty cut marred his bottom lip.

'Elijah,' Caroline said, her voice barely above a whisper. 'What on earth happened?'

Elijah attempted a smile, wincing as the movement pulled at his split lip. 'Morning, boss. Bit of a rough weekend, I'm afraid.'

Caroline ushered him towards her office, away from the prying eyes of their colleagues. She closed the door behind them, gesturing for Elijah to take a seat.

'Elijah, what happened?' she asked, her tone a mixture of concern and authority.

Elijah sank into the chair, his usual confident demeanour replaced by something more vulnerable. He ran a hand through his hair, wincing again as he brushed against a tender spot on his scalp.

'I'm sorry, boss,' he said, his voice low. 'I can't talk about it.'

Caroline leaned against her desk, arms folded. 'Can't or won't?'

'Both, I suppose,' Elijah replied, not meeting her eyes.

'Elijah, I need to know what happened,' Caroline pressed, her voice low but firm. 'I've got a duty of care to you.'

Elijah's fingers drummed an erratic rhythm on the desk. The sound seemed to echo in the tense silence of Caroline's office. 'I told you, boss. I can't—'

A sharp buzz cut through the tension. Elijah snatched his phone from his pocket, his good eye scanning the screen. Something flickered across his face – triumph? Fear? – before vanishing behind a mask of neutrality.

'Sorry, I've got to go,' he muttered, already half out of his chair. 'Meeting with Professional Standards about... this.' He gestured vaguely at his face.

Caroline felt more confused and concerned than ever. Before she could speak again, Elijah was gone, the door swinging shut behind him with a soft click. The sudden exit left Caroline feeling wrong-footed, a sensation she wasn't accustomed to and didn't appreciate.

Caroline stared at the empty doorway, a nagging sense of unease settling in her stomach. Something wasn't right, but she couldn't put her finger on what. She'd known Elijah for only a short time, but this evasiveness seemed out of character for the usually forthright detective.

She moved to the doorway of her office, looking out over the CID office. The familiar sounds of the office slowly filtered back in – the gentle hum of computers, the rustle of papers, the quiet murmur of conversation. Sara and Aidan exchanged glances, clearly as perplexed by Elijah's behaviour as she was.

'Did either of you speak to Elijah this morning?' Caroline asked, trying to keep her tone casual.

Aidan shook his head. 'He was already in your office when I arrived. Didn't even say good morning. But boss, his face... What happened to him?'

Caroline sighed, running a hand through her hair. 'I wish I knew. He's being frustratingly tight-lipped about it.'

Minutes ticked by, each second amplifying the strange atmosphere that had descended upon the room. Caroline had just decided to call Elijah when the door swung open again.

Dexter strode in, his brow furrowed in concentration as he scrolled through something on his phone. He glanced up, nodding a distracted greeting to his colleagues before settling at his desk. The normality of his entrance felt almost jarring after the tension of the morning.

'Morning, all,' he said, reaching for his mouse. 'Any breaks in Operation Helix over the weekend?'

The lack of response made him look up, his eyes narrowing as he took in the tense expressions around him. 'What's going on? Did something happen?'

Caroline opened her mouth to respond, but before she could form the words, the office door burst open once more. Three men in suits entered, their stern expressions and purposeful strides marking them as anything but ordinary visitors.

The tallest of the three, a man with dyed-black hair and a face like carved granite, stepped forward. His presence seemed to suck the air out of the room. 'Detective Sergeant Antoine?'

Dexter rose slowly, confusion etched across his features. 'Yes, that's me. Can I help you?'

'I'm Detective Chief Inspector Rawlings from EMSOU.' The man's voice carried the weight of authority. 'I'm here to place you under arrest on suspicion of causing grievous bodily harm with intent.'

A collective gasp rippled through the office. Caroline felt as though the floor had suddenly tilted beneath her feet. She gripped the doorframe of her office, steadying herself against the shock.

'What?' Dexter's voice was barely above a whisper. 'This has to be some kind of mistake.'

DCI Rawlings continued, his tone brooking no argument. 'You do not have to say anything, but it may harm your defence if you do not mention when questioned something which you later rely on in court. Anything you do say may be given in evidence.'

As one of the other officers moved to handcuff Dexter, chaos erupted in the office. Aidan half-rose from his chair, his face a mask of shock. 'This can't be right,' he protested. 'Dexter wouldn't—'

Aidan's coffee mug slipped from his grasp, shattering on the floor and sending dark liquid seeping across the linoleum. The crash seemed to jolt everyone into action.

Caroline found her voice at last, years of training kicking in despite her shock. 'DCI Rawlings, surely this can't be necessary. Detective Sergeant Antoine is a respected member of this team. There must be some misunderstanding.'

Rawlings turned to her, his expression softening fractionally. 'I'm sorry, DI Hills, but we need to conduct our inquiries. DS Antoine will be taken in for questioning immediately.'

'What inquiries?' Dexter repeated, his voice hoarse. 'I haven't done anything!'

Caroline's mind raced. Elijah's battered face, his

evasiveness, the sudden appearance of EMSOU officers...
It was all connected, but how?

'Dexter,' she said, fighting to keep her voice steady,
'don't say anything more. We'll sort this out.'

As the officers led a shell-shocked Dexter towards the
door, Caroline caught a glimpse of movement in the
corridor. Elijah stood just outside, his battered face an
unsettling mixture of satisfaction and something that
might have been regret.

Their eyes met for a brief moment before Elijah
turned away, disappearing down the hallway as quickly as
he'd appeared. The sight of him sent a chill down
Caroline's spine. What game was he playing?

The office door closed behind Dexter and the
EMSOU officers, leaving a stunned silence in their wake.
Caroline surveyed her team, noting the mix of confusion
and disbelief on most faces. Sara, however, remained
oddly still, her expression carefully neutral.

Aidan was the first to break the silence. 'Boss, this is
insane. Dexter wouldn't hurt a fly, let alone assault Elijah.'

Caroline held up a hand, silencing the growing
murmurs. 'I know you all have questions. So do I. But
right now, we need to focus on our jobs and let them do
theirs.'

'But it doesn't make any sense,' Aidan protested.
'Dexter and Elijah were getting on better lately. They even
went for a drink together on Saturday night.'

Caroline glanced at Sara, noticing her continued
silence. 'Sara, you've been quiet. Any thoughts?'

Sara shrugged, her face a mask of professionalism. 'I'm just trying to process it all, boss. It's a lot to take in.'

Caroline nodded slowly, a niggling suspicion forming in the back of her mind. She pushed it aside for now, focusing on the immediate problem. 'Right. For now, we carry on with Operation Helix as best we can. Aidan, I want you to take point on Dexter's ongoing cases. Sara, you'll assist him.'

Both detectives nodded, though Aidan still looked shaken.

'What about you, boss?' Aidan asked.

Caroline's jaw set in a determined line. 'I'm going to speak with the Chief Superintendent. We need to know where we stand with this investigation now that Dexter's been arrested.'

As her team set to work, Caroline retreated to her office, closing the door behind her. She sank into her chair, the events of the morning replaying in her mind. The arrest of one of her own had shaken the foundations of her team, and the tremors threatened to destabilise Operation Helix entirely.

She reached for her phone, her fingers hovering over the keypad. There were calls to be made, explanations to be given, but the weight of responsibility pressed down on her like a physical force. Each number dialled would set off a chain reaction, pulling threads that might unravel more than just this case.

As she punched in the Chief Superintendent's number, Caroline couldn't shake the image of Elijah's face from her mind - not just the bruises that marked it, but the fleeting expression she'd glimpsed as Dexter was led away. It was a discordant note in the symphony of their investigation, a jarring reminder that sometimes the greatest mysteries lay not in the cases they solved, but in the people who solved them.

The line connected, and Caroline straightened in her chair. 'Sir,' she said, her voice steady despite the turmoil in her gut. 'We have a situation with Operation Helix. I need your guidance.'

As she began to outline the morning's events, Caroline's free hand reached for the case file. Whatever had transpired between Dexter and Elijah, she knew one thing for certain: Emily Ashcroft's killer was still out there. And now, more than ever, they needed to stay focused on bringing that person to justice.

27

Caroline stood at the front of the incident room, her hands gripping the back of a chair so tightly her knuckles had turned white. The faces of her team stared back at her, a mixture of shock, disbelief, and confusion etched across their features.

'I know this is... difficult to process,' she began, her voice steadier than she felt. 'But we need to focus on the facts.'

Aidan's hand shot up. 'Boss, there's got to be some mistake. Dexter wouldn't—'

'I know, Aidan,' Caroline cut him off, perhaps more sharply than she'd intended. She took a deep breath, forcing herself to slow down. 'We all know Dexter. But right now, we have to let Leicestershire Police conduct their investigation.'

A heavy silence fell over the room. Caroline's gaze

swept over her team, noting their reactions. Aidan looked ready to argue further, his jaw clenched tight. Most of the others wore expressions of stunned disbelief. Only Sara seemed... different. Caroline couldn't quite put her finger on it, but the young detective's reaction seemed somehow muted compared to the others.

The door opened, and Elijah limped in. His battered face drew gasps from those who hadn't seen him earlier. He moved gingerly to an empty chair, lowering himself into it with a barely suppressed groan.

'Elijah,' Caroline said, fighting to keep her voice neutral. 'Are you sure you should be here? You need to rest.'

Elijah shook his head, wincing at the movement. 'No, I... I need to explain. You all deserve to know what happened.'

Caroline noticed Sara shift in her seat, her eyes fixed on the floor. Something about her body language set off a warning bell in Caroline's mind, but she pushed the thought aside for now.

'It was after we left the pub,' Elijah began, his voice quiet but carrying clearly in the silent room. 'I thought we'd had a good evening, cleared the air. But then...' He paused, swallowing hard. 'Dexter followed me. He was angry, saying I was trying to take over his case, that I didn't know my place.'

Aidan made a noise of disbelief, but Caroline silenced him with a look.

Elijah continued, his good eye glistening with what

looked like unshed tears. 'I tried to calm him down, but he wouldn't listen. He grabbed my cricket bat off me – I don't know why. I remember thinking how strange that was, and then...' He gestured vaguely at his face. 'The next thing I knew, I was waking up in hospital.'

The room erupted into murmurs. Caroline raised her hands, calling for quiet. 'I know this is a lot to take in,' she said, her mind racing. 'But we can't let this derail our investigation. Emily Ashcroft's killer is still out there, and we owe it to her to stay focused.'

As she spoke, Caroline caught a flicker of movement from the corner of her eye. Aidan was staring at Sara, his brow furrowed in confusion. Sara, for her part, was studiously avoiding eye contact with anyone in the room.

Caroline filed the observation away for later. Right now, she had a team to lead and an investigation to salvage.

'I'll take over as Acting SIO on Op Helix,' she said, her tone brooking no argument. 'Aidan, you'll assist me. Elijah and Sara, carry on with your assigned tasks. We'll have a full briefing this afternoon to reassess our progress on Operation Helix.'

As the team began to disperse, murmuring amongst themselves, Caroline's gaze was drawn back to Elijah. For just a moment, she thought she saw something flicker across his battered face – a hint of satisfaction, quickly masked by a grimace of pain.

Caroline shook her head, pushing the thought away.

She was letting her emotions cloud her judgment. Elijah was the victim here. Wasn't he?

As she headed back to her office, Caroline couldn't shake the feeling that she was missing something crucial. But what? And more importantly, how was she going to hold her team together in the face of this crisis?

28

Dexter stood in his cell, motionless for a moment, his mind still reeling from the events of the morning.

How had he gone from heading into work on a Monday to being arrested for GBH?

He sank onto the thin mattress of the cell's narrow bed, his head in his hands. The urge to punch something, to scream, to rage against the injustice of it all was almost overwhelming. But he forced himself to take deep breaths, to maintain control. He couldn't afford to lose his temper now. That's exactly what they'd expect from someone guilty of assault.

As his initial shock began to subside, anger seeped in to take its place. Elijah. The bastard had set him up. He could see it now, all the pieces falling into place. The invite for a drink, the insistence on that particular pub in the middle of nowhere, the seemingly friendly conversation. It had all been a carefully orchestrated plan.

Dexter's mind raced back to Friday night. He'd been surprised when Elijah had suggested they go for a pint, but he'd agreed readily enough. It had seemed like a chance to clear the air, to move past their initial friction and work together more effectively on Operation Helix.

Saturday had been a pleasant enough evening. They'd talked about work, about their backgrounds, even shared a few laughs over a couple of pints.

Dexter shook his head, trying to clear the fog of disbelief. He'd left the pub around ten o'clock, he was sure of it. Elijah had been fine then, a bit tipsy perhaps, but certainly not injured. Dexter had driven home along winding country lanes, the headlights of his car cutting through the darkness.

With a jolt, Dexter realised why Elijah had chosen that particular pub. No ANPR cameras on those back roads. No way to prove definitively when he'd left or where he'd gone. It was clever. Too clever.

A wave of nausea washed over him as the full implications of his situation became clear. Elijah had friends in EMSOU. That was made clear by how quickly the arrest had been made. But who could Dexter trust? Who would believe him over one of their own?

The sound of footsteps in the corridor outside his cell snapped Dexter out of his spiralling thoughts. Keys jangled, and the cell door swung open.

'Antoine,' the officer said, his face impassive. 'Interview room. Your Fed rep and solicitor are here.'

Dexter nodded, standing up slowly. He took another deep breath, squaring his shoulders. He was innocent. He just had to stay calm and tell the truth. Somehow, he had to find a way to prove that Elijah was lying.

As he followed the officer down the corridor, Dexter steeled himself for what was to come. Whatever game Elijah was playing, Dexter was determined not to be the fall guy. He'd find a way to expose the truth, no matter what it took.

The interview room was small and stark. A recording device sat in the centre, its red light blinking steadily. Dexter took a seat, nodding gratefully to the man and woman already seated on his side of the table.

'DS Antoine,' came the greeting from Dexter's appointed Police Federation representative.

'Joe, bloody hell,' Dexter said, shaking him warmly by the hand. 'It's good to see you again. Rather it wasn't like this, mind, but hey.'

Joe Lloyd had been a familiar face on the streets of Oakham for a number of years as Rutland's local beat bobby, before taking on his new role with the Police Federation.

'We'll get through it in the best way we can,' Joe said, his voice low and reassuring. 'And this is Sarah Patel, your solicitor.'

Dexter shook their hands, trying to ignore the tremor

in his own. 'Thank you for coming,' he managed, his throat dry.

The door opened again, and two plainclothes officers entered. The older of the two, a man with greying hair and piercing blue eyes, took a seat opposite Dexter. His companion, a younger woman with her dark hair pulled back in a severe bun, sat beside him.

'I'm Detective Inspector James Harding,' the man said, his tone clipped and professional. 'This is Detective Sergeant Lisa Chen. We'll be conducting this interview. For the benefit of the tape, it's now 14:23 on Monday, 29th July.'

DI Harding leaned forward, his gaze locked on Dexter. 'DS Antoine, you've been arrested on suspicion of assaulting Detective Sergeant Elijah Drummond late on Saturday night in the village of Wymeswold. Do you understand?'

Dexter nodded, then remembered to speak for the tape. 'Yes, I understand.'

'Before we begin,' Sarah Patel interjected, 'I'd like to state for the record that my client categorically denies these allegations and will be cooperating fully with your investigation.'

DI Harding acknowledged this with a curt nod. 'Very well. DS Antoine, can you tell us where you were on Saturday evening?'

Dexter took a deep breath. 'I was at The Three Crowns pub in Wymeswold with DS Drummond. We'd gone for a drink.'

'Why's that?' Harding asked.

Dexter sighed. 'Because we hadn't been getting on all that well, and we thought we'd bury the hatchet.'

'I see. Whose idea was that?'

'It was his,' Dexter replied.

Harding nodded slowly, his slight smirk telling Dexter all he needed to know. 'And what time did you leave the pub?'

'Around ten o'clock, I think. Maybe a couple of minutes after.'

DS Chen spoke up, her voice cool. 'And where did you go after leaving the pub?'

'I drove straight home,' Dexter replied. 'It was late, and I had a lot to do the next day.'

'Can anyone confirm your movements after leaving the pub?' DI Harding asked.

Dexter hesitated, knowing how his answer would sound. 'No,' he admitted. 'I drove home alone on the country lanes. There wouldn't be any cameras on that route.'

He saw the detectives exchange a glance and felt his heart sink. It sounded weak, even to his own ears.

'DS Antoine,' DI Harding continued, 'DS Drummond has given us a statement. He claims that after leaving the pub, you confronted him in the car park.'

Dexter's jaw clenched. 'That's not true,' he said, fighting to keep his voice level. 'I left Elijah – DS Drummond – at the pub. He was fine when I left. I didn't see him again or confront him about anything.'

'DS Drummond's statement is quite detailed,' DS Chen said, her tone sceptical. 'He claims you said, and I quote, "You think you can just waltz in and take over my case? I'll show you what happens to cocky little upstarts who don't know their place."'

Dexter felt a surge of anger. 'I never said anything like that! It doesn't even sound like me! This is ridiculous. Elijah and I had our differences at first, sure, but we'd moved past that. That's why we went for a drink in the first place.'

'Yet DS Drummond ended up severely beaten and identified you as his attacker,' DI Harding pointed out. 'We have his statement, we have physical evidence—'

'What physical evidence?' Dexter interrupted, before glancing at his solicitor apologetically.

Sarah Patel leaned in. 'My client has a right to know what evidence you're claiming to have against him.'

DI Harding's lips thinned, but he nodded. 'We recovered the weapon used in the assault. A cricket bat. It has DS Drummond's blood on it, as well as your fingerprints, DS Antoine.'

Dexter felt the blood drain from his face. 'A cricket bat?'

'Yes,' DS Chen confirmed, her eyes narrowing. 'Are you saying you're not familiar with this item?'

Dexter's mind raced. He remembered now – Elijah showing him his cricket bat at the pub, regaling him with tales of village matches. He'd held it, mimicked a few strokes. His fingerprints would be all over it.

'I... I did handle a cricket bat at the pub,' Dexter said slowly, aware of how damning this admission might sound. 'Elijah was showing it to me. We were just talking about cricket.'

'A convenient explanation,' DI Harding said, his tone dripping with disbelief.

Joe Lloyd spoke up. 'I think we need to take a break,' he said firmly. 'My colleague needs a moment to collect his thoughts.'

DI Harding looked like he wanted to object, but after a moment, he nodded. 'We'll take ten minutes,' he said, standing up. 'For the tape, the time is 14:26, and we're suspending the interview.'

As the detectives left the room, Dexter slumped in his chair, his head spinning. How had Elijah managed to twist everything so perfectly? The cricket bat, the lack of witnesses, the fabricated confrontation – it was all so neatly arranged against him.

'Dexter,' Sarah Patel said gently, 'I need you to focus. We need to go through your movements that night in detail. Every little thing you remember could be important.'

Dexter nodded, trying to push down the rising tide of despair. As he began to recount the events of Saturday night, he couldn't shake the feeling that he was caught in a trap with no way out. Somewhere out there, Elijah was probably laughing, watching as Dexter's life and career crumbled around him.

But as he spoke, a small spark of determination

flickered to life in Dexter's chest. He was innocent. And somehow, some way, he would prove it. Because if Elijah had gone to these lengths to frame him, who knew what else he might be capable of?

29

The incident room slowly emptied, a subdued murmur replacing the usual chatter. Aidan remained at his desk, mechanically sorting through papers without really seeing them. His mind kept replaying Elijah's account, searching for... something. A detail out of place, a note that didn't quite ring true.

He glanced up, catching sight of Sara across the room. She was packing up her things, her movements precise and controlled. Too controlled, he realised. While everyone else still looked shell-shocked, Sara's face was a mask of careful neutrality.

That was it. That was what had been nagging at him.

Aidan watched her for a moment longer, noting the tight set of her shoulders, the way her eyes didn't quite meet anyone else's. A theory began to form in his mind, but he needed more. He needed to talk to her.

He approached her desk, trying to keep his voice casual. 'Fancy a brew?'

Sara looked up, startled. For a split second, something flashed in her eyes – panic? – before it was quickly suppressed. 'Oh, um, sure. Thanks, Aidan.'

They made their way to the kitchenette in silence. Aidan's mind raced, trying to piece together the puzzle that was Sara's behaviour. As he filled the kettle, he watched her from the corner of his eye. She leaned against the counter, arms crossed, staring at nothing in particular.

'So,' Aidan began, keeping his tone light as he reached for mugs, 'bit of a shock, all that, wasn't it?'

Sara nodded, not quite meeting his eyes. 'Yeah, awful business.'

'I can't believe it about Dexter,' Aidan pressed on, studying her reaction. 'I mean, who'd have thought he had it in him?'

Sara's fingers tightened on her arms. 'I suppose you never really know someone.'

The kettle clicked off. Aidan poured water into the mugs, buying himself time to formulate his next question. The rich aroma of tea filled the small space, a comforting scent at odds with the growing tension.

'Thing is,' he said, handing her a mug, 'you didn't seem all that shocked.'

Her head snapped up, eyes wide. 'What do you mean?'

'Well, everyone else was gobsmacked. But you...' Aidan paused, choosing his words carefully. 'You barely reacted at all.'

Sara's fingers tightened around the mug. 'I was shocked. I just... I don't know, I guess I process things differently.'

Aidan leaned back against the opposite counter, creating space between them. He took a sip of his tea, using the moment to observe Sara. She was staring into her mug, avoiding his gaze.

'See, I've been thinking about it,' he continued, keeping his voice neutral. 'And I can't help but wonder: do you not believe Elijah?'

'Of course I believe him,' Sara said quickly. Too quickly. 'Why wouldn't I?'

'Then why no shock? No outrage?' Aidan set his mug down, crossing his arms. 'Dexter's our colleague, our friend. This should be devastating news.'

Sara fumbled with her mug, nearly spilling tea. 'I... I suppose I've just noticed things about Dexter lately. His behaviour, you know?'

Aidan raised an eyebrow, waiting for her to continue.

Sara took a deep breath. 'I hate to say it, but I wouldn't be that surprised if he'd done something like this. He always seemed to have it in him, deep down.'

The words hung in the air between them. Aidan felt a flicker of disappointment, quickly replaced by a surge of certainty. He'd known Sara for years, worked closely with her. He knew when she was lying.

'That's bollocks, Sara,' he said quietly, 'and you know it.'

Sara's face flushed. 'Excuse me?'

'Dexter's one of the most level-headed blokes I know.' Aidan pushed off from the counter, taking a step towards her. 'You've never had a bad word to say about him before today.'

Sara set her mug down with a clatter, tea sloshing over the rim. 'People change, Aidan. You don't know everything about everyone.'

'No,' Aidan agreed, 'I don't. But I know you, Sara. And I know when you're not telling the truth.'

The colour drained from Sara's face. For a moment, Aidan felt a pang of... something. Hurt? Jealousy? He pushed the feeling aside, focusing on the task at hand.

'I think I know why you reacted the way you did,' he continued, the pieces falling into place as he spoke. 'You already knew what had happened.'

Sara's eyes widened. 'That's ridiculous. How could I possibly—'

'The only way you could have known,' Aidan interrupted, his voice low and intense, 'is if you were close to Elijah outside of work.'

Sara took a step back, bumping into the counter behind her. 'I don't know what you're talking about.'

'Come off it, Sara.' Aidan shook his head, a mixture of frustration and something like betrayal churning in his gut. 'It's obvious now that I think about it. The way you two interact, the little glances, how you always seem to know what he's thinking.'

He paused, steeling himself for the question he didn't really want to ask. 'How long has it been going on?'

Sara's demeanour shifted from defensive to cold. 'You're out of line, Aidan. My personal life is none of your business.'

'It is when it affects the job,' Aidan shot back. 'If you and Elijah are... involved, and you knew about this before the rest of us, that's a serious breach of—'

'Stop,' Sara interrupted, holding up a hand. 'Just stop. You don't know what you're talking about.'

They stared at each other for a long moment, the air thick with unspoken words. Aidan could see the struggle playing out behind Sara's eyes. She knew she'd been caught out, but she wasn't going to admit it.

The silence stretched between them, broken only by the distant sounds of the office beyond the kitchenette door. Aidan waited, giving Sara the chance to come clean, to explain. But she remained silent, her face a mixture of defiance and fear.

Finally, Sara spoke, her voice barely above a whisper. 'Aidan, please. Whatever you think you know, or suspect... don't repeat it to anyone else. Please.'

The plea hung in the air, heavy with implication. Aidan opened his mouth to respond, but Sara was already brushing past him, leaving her untouched mug of tea on the counter. He watched her go, a whirlwind of emotions churning in his gut.

As the kitchenette door swung shut behind her, Aidan was left alone with his thoughts, and a decision to make.

30

Derek Parsons zipped up his lightweight jacket as he set off down the woodland path, his border collie Meg trotting ahead, nose to the ground. The afternoon sun filtered through the canopy, casting dappled shadows on the ground. A gentle breeze rustled the leaves, carrying the earthy scent of the woods.

He'd taken this route every day for the past fifteen years, rain or shine. It was his favourite part of the day – just him, Meg, and the peaceful woodland surrounding them.

Derek paused to pick up a fallen branch, tossing it off the trail. He'd always been a stickler for keeping the paths clear, much to his wife Sandra's amusement. 'You're fighting a losing battle,' she'd tell him with a fond smile. But Derek couldn't help himself. It was ingrained in him, this need to maintain order in his little corner of the world.

As they rounded a bend in the trail, Derek noticed Meg had stopped, her tail straight and ears perked forward. 'What is it, girl?' he called out, quickening his pace to catch up. His knees protested slightly – a reminder that he wasn't as young as he used to be.

Meg turned to look at him, then back at something in the undergrowth. She let out a low whine, pawing at the ground nervously. Derek frowned. This was unusual behaviour for his normally exuberant companion. As he drew closer, he noticed a peculiar smell – something beyond the usual woodland scents. Something... wrong.

'Meg, come,' he commanded, suddenly wary. But Meg didn't budge. Instead, she began to dig at the pile of leaves and branches just off the path. Derek's unease grew. In all their years of walking these trails, he'd never seen Meg act like this.

A sense of foreboding settled in Derek's stomach. He'd read enough crime novels to know where this was going, but surely that sort of thing didn't happen in real life. Not here in their quiet little corner of the world. This was Rutland, for heaven's sake. The biggest excitement they usually had was a lost sheep or a minor traffic accident in Oakham.

'Meg, stop that,' he said, his voice lacking conviction. He took a few hesitant steps forward, peering into the undergrowth. The smell was stronger now, sickeningly sweet and unmistakably... off.

That's when he saw it. A pale hand, partially obscured by leaves and dirt, fingers curled as if grasping at the earth. Derek stumbled backwards, his heart pounding. 'Oh God,' he whispered, fumbling for his mobile phone with shaking hands.

As he dialled 999, his eyes remained fixed on that terrible sight. He could see more now – a strand of dark hair, the curve of a shoulder. Whoever it was, they'd made a poor job of hiding the body. Derek's mind reeled. How long had it been here? Had he walked past it yesterday, oblivious?

'Emergency services, which service do you require?' The operator's calm voice seemed bizarrely out of place in that moment.

'Police,' Derek managed to croak out. 'I've... I've found a body.'

'I'm sorry, sir, did you say you've found a body?'

'Yes,' Derek replied, his voice steadier now. 'In Burley Wood. Uh, I'm not quite sure how to describe the exact spot.'

'It's okay, we can use your mobile phone's location to direct the officers.'

The rest of the conversation passed in a blur. Derek answered the operator's questions mechanically, his mind struggling to process what he was seeing. Yes, he was certain it was a body. No, he hadn't touched anything. Yes, he would stay where he was until the police arrived.

As he ended the call, Derek found himself rooted to the spot, staring blankly at the partially hidden form. Time seemed to stand still. The woodland around him faded away, leaving only the pale hand and that sickly-sweet smell. He didn't know how long he stood there, paralysed by shock. It could have been minutes or hours.

Meg's whine eventually brought him back to reality. The dog pressed against his leg, sensing his distress. Derek absently patted her head, his eyes still fixed on the gruesome discovery.

His thoughts raced. Who was she? He was certain it was a woman, though he couldn't say why. Perhaps it was the delicate curve of the visible wrist, or the length of the dark hair he could see peeking out from beneath the leaves.

More importantly, who could have done this? Derek had lived in Rutland all his life. He knew most of the locals, at least by sight. The idea that one of them could be capable of... this... it was almost inconceivable.

Yet here was the proof, lying just a few feet away from where he stood.

The peaceful woodland suddenly felt oppressive, full of shadows and secrets. Every rustle of leaves, every snapping twig made Derek start. He shivered, drawing Meg close.

Derek's mind wandered to Pauline, probably at home preparing dinner, blissfully unaware of what he'd stumbled upon. How would he tell her? Should he tell her? The thought of bringing this darkness into their home, tainting their quiet life with the knowledge of such violence, made his stomach churn.

He glanced at his watch, surprised to see that nearly fifteen minutes had passed since he'd made the call. Where were the police? Surely they should have arrived by now.

As if on cue, he heard the distant rumble of vehicles approaching.

Relief washed over him, quickly followed by a fresh wave of anxiety. This was real. In a few moments, this quiet stretch of woodland would be swarming with police. There would be questions, statements to give. And soon, everyone in Rutland would know.

As the sound of car doors slamming reached him, Derek took one last look at the partially hidden form in the undergrowth. 'I'm sorry,' he whispered, though he wasn't sure who he was apologising to – the victim, or himself.

The sound of voices and approaching footsteps jolted Derek back to the present. He straightened up, trying to compose himself. Meg's ears pricked up at the noise.

Derek Parsons had a feeling their quiet little world was about to change forever. As the first police officer came into view, he took a deep breath, steeling himself for what was to come.

31

Caroline stifled a yawn as she settled at her desk, the early morning quiet of the station broken only by the gentle hum of computers and the distant chatter of the front desk. She'd barely taken her first sip of coffee when Derek Arnold's voice boomed across the bullpen.

'Hills! My office, now!'

The urgency in his tone made Caroline's stomach clench. She set down her mug and made her way to Arnold's office, acutely aware of the curious glances from her colleagues.

Arnold was standing behind his desk, his face a storm cloud of fury. Without a word, he turned his laptop round and thrust it at her.

Caroline's eyes widened as she took in the garish headline:

COPPER CLOBBERS COLLEAGUE: RUTLAND POLICE DESCEND INTO CHAOS.

'What the hell is this?' she demanded, scanning the article with growing disbelief and anger.

Arnold's voice was low and dangerous. 'That, Hills, is Leah MacGregor making us look like complete bloody idiots. And at the worst possible time.'

Caroline's grip on the paper tightened, her knuckles turning white. 'This is absurd. She's practically accusing Dexter of attempted murder!'

'Oh, it gets better,' Arnold said, his tone dripping with sarcasm. 'Keep reading.'

As Caroline delved deeper into the article, her anger gave way to a cold, sinking feeling. MacGregor had woven a tale of departmental discord, hinting at cover-ups and internal power struggles. Somehow, she'd got hold of details about Elijah's injuries that shouldn't have been public knowledge.

'How did she get this information?' Caroline asked, looking up from the paper.

Arnold's laugh was mirthless. 'That's what I'd like to know. We've got a leak, Hills. And it's making us look like a bunch of incompetent thugs who can't even keep our own house in order.'

He sank into his chair, suddenly looking every one of his years. 'Do you have any idea how bad this is? We're in the middle of a high-profile murder investigation. And now this?'

Caroline opened her mouth to defend Dexter, but Arnold cut her off with a sharp gesture.

'I don't want to hear it. I don't care if Antoine did it or not. What I care about is that this story is out there, making us all look like fools.'

'But sir—'

'No buts,' Arnold snapped. 'You need to get this under control. Find the leak. Shut MacGregor down. And for God's sake, make some progress on the actual case.'

Caroline bristled at his tone. 'We are making progress. If you'd just let me explain—'

'Explain?' Arnold's voice rose. 'Explain what? How you've got officers assaulting each other? How you're running this investigation like it's your own personal crusade?'

The accusation stung, but Caroline held her ground. 'My methods get results, sir. You know that.'

'Your methods are going to get us all sacked if you're not careful,' Arnold retorted. He took a deep breath, visibly trying to calm himself. 'Look, Caroline. You're a good detective. But you can't keep operating like you're above the rules. Not with MacGregor breathing down our necks.'

Caroline nodded stiffly, knowing there was no point in arguing further. 'What do you want me to do?'

'Damage control,' Arnold said firmly. 'Find out how MacGregor got her information. And Caroline? Whatever you do, do it by the book. We can't afford any more slip-ups.'

As Caroline turned to leave, Arnold added, 'And keep Antoine away from this investigation. Suspended means suspended, understood?'

'Yes, sir,' Caroline replied, her tone carefully neutral.

She left Arnold's office, her mind racing. The office had filled up during their meeting, and she could feel the weight of her team's gazes. They'd all seen the article by now, she was sure.

Caroline strode to her desk, snatching up her now-cold coffee. As she gulped it down, her eyes fell on the case board. Emily's face smiled back at her, a stark reminder of what was really at stake here.

Leah MacGregor's article was a complication, yes. But it didn't change the facts. Somewhere out there, a killer was walking free.

Caroline set down her mug with a decisive thunk. She turned to face her team, noting the mix of concern and determination on their faces. 'Alright, listen up,' she said, her voice carrying across the suddenly quiet room.

'I know you've all seen the article. But right now, we can't afford to be distracted.' She paused, making eye contact with each member of her team. 'Aidan, I want you to go through every piece of evidence we have on Emily's murder. Leave no stone unturned. Cross-reference everything, see if we've missed any connections.'

'What about Dexter?' Sara asked, her voice quiet but firm.

Caroline felt a pang of guilt. 'Dexter's suspension

stands for now. We can't risk giving MacGregor any more ammunition.'

She saw the flash of disappointment in Sara's eyes, but there was nothing to be done about it. 'As for the rest of you, I need every scrap of information we have on Environmental Waste Management Solutions. Financials, personnel records, waste disposal logs – everything.'

The team began to disperse, a renewed sense of purpose in their movements. Caroline turned back to her desk, her mind already mapping out her next moves.

A soft cough made her look up. Elijah stood there, his face still bearing the marks of his alleged assault. 'What about me, boss?'

Caroline studied him for a moment, weighing her options. She thought back to what Dexter had told her about Elijah and Leah's conversation in the car park. 'I need you to go through all of Leah MacGregor's recent articles. Look for patterns, recurring sources, anything that might give us a clue about her informant.'

Elijah nodded, a determined glint in his eye. 'On it.'

As he walked away, Caroline sank into her chair, the weight of the situation settling heavily on her shoulders. She knew she should be focusing on the murders, on the environmental crimes, but MacGregor's article had thrown a spanner in the works. They needed to plug the leak, and fast. She had her suspicions, but she needed them confirmed.

She pulled out her notebook, jotting down ideas for damage control. A press conference? No, too risky without more information. A formal complaint against MacGregor? That could backfire spectacularly.

Caroline rubbed her temples, feeling the beginnings of a headache. She glanced at the clock – not even noon, and already the day felt endless.

Just then, her phone buzzed. A text from Mark.

Saw the article. You okay? X

She smiled despite herself, appreciating his concern.

Hanging in there. Might be a late one
tonight x

Putting her phone away, Caroline took a deep breath. One problem at a time, she reminded herself. First, find the leak. Then, deal with MacGregor. And through it all, keep pushing forward on the case.

She stood up, stretching out the kinks in her back. As she surveyed the bustling office, she felt a familiar surge of determination. They'd weather this storm, just like they had every other challenge.

32

Aidan's palms were clammy as he pushed open the heavy oak door of the Three Crowns. He was well out of his jurisdiction, and the last thing he needed was to get pulled up on that. But this lead was too important to ignore, even if it meant bending the rules a bit.

The familiar smell of beer and pub grub greeted him as he stepped inside. The lunchtime rush had passed, leaving only a handful of regulars nursing their pints at the bar. Aidan approached the barman, a stocky fellow with greying temples and a well-worn apron.

'Afternoon,' Aidan said, trying to keep his voice steady as he flashed his warrant card. 'Detective Constable Chilcott. I was hoping to have a quick chat about Saturday night, if that's alright?'

The barman's eyes narrowed slightly as he glanced at the warrant card. 'Rutland Police? Bit far from home, aren't you?'

Aidan felt his heart rate pick up. 'Ah. Yes. The case I'm working on involves some Rutland officers, so I'm following up on a lead here. You the landlord, are you?' he asked, hoping to change the subject.

The man nodded, seemingly satisfied with the explanation. 'That's right. Name's Bill. What can I help you with, mate?'

Aidan leaned against the bar, keeping his voice low. 'I'm looking into the incident that occurred on Saturday night. There were two men in here – one in cricket whites, the other in plain clothes. Do you remember them?'

Bill's brow furrowed in concentration. 'Yeah, I do. The cricket lad's the one who got done over in the car park, right? A regular – Elijah, I think. The other fella was new. Black guy. Seemed a bit on edge, if you ask me.'

Aidan's pulse quickened, but he kept his face neutral. 'Can you tell me what time they left?'

'The new fella left around ten, give or take. Elijah stayed to finish his pint.'

'Did you notice anything unusual about their behaviour?'

Bill shook his head. 'Not really. They were laughing and joking most of the night. The new guy even had a go with Elijah's cricket bat.'

Aidan raised an eyebrow. 'Oh?'

'Yeah, nothing aggressive like. Just swinging it about, showing off a bit. Careful not to hit anyone, mind.'

Aidan nodded, jotting notes in his pocket book. 'And

after the other man left, did Elijah say or do anything out of the ordinary?'

Bill shrugged. 'Not that I noticed. He finished his pint and headed out. Said he was walking home.'

'Thanks, Bill. Mind if I have a look at your CCTV footage from that night?'

'Again? Your colleagues have already taken copies.'

'Yeah, sorry,' Aidan replied. 'Probably won't surprise you to learn things aren't always as organised as they should be at our end.'

'You can say that again. Right, this way,' Bill said, gesturing towards a door marked 'Private' behind the bar. 'The system's upstairs in my flat.'

Aidan followed Bill through a narrow corridor and up a creaky staircase. The walls were lined with framed photographs, mostly of cricket teams spanning several decades.

'You're big on cricket around here, then?' Aidan asked, nodding towards the photos.

Bill chuckled. 'Oh yes, it's a religion in these parts. That's why your man Elijah fits right in. He's a decent player, from what I hear.'

They reached the landing, and Bill fumbled with a set of keys before opening the door to his flat. The living space was small but tidy, with a worn leather sofa facing an old TV set. In the corner, a desk held a computer monitor and a mess of wires.

'Sorry about the clutter,' Bill said, moving towards the desk. 'The missus is always on at me to tidy up a bit.'

Aidan waved away the apology. 'No worries. I appreciate you letting me take a look.'

Bill settled into the desk chair with a grunt, tapping at the keyboard. 'Now then, let's see. Saturday night, you said?'

Aidan nodded, leaning in to get a better view of the screen. 'That's right. Around half nine to half ten, if you can.'

Bill navigated through the system, muttering to himself as he searched for the right time stamp. 'Here we go,' he said finally, bringing up the footage of the main bar area.

Aidan watched intently as the grainy images flickered to life. He could make out Dexter and Elijah seated at a corner table, their body language relaxed and friendly.

'Can we fast forward a bit?' Aidan asked. 'I'm particularly interested in when they left.'

Bill obliged, and they watched as the evening progressed at high speed. Aidan's eyes were fixed on Dexter and Elijah, noting their interactions and movements.

'Stop,' Aidan said suddenly. 'Can you play it from here?'

Bill slowed the footage back to normal speed. On screen, Dexter was standing, cricket bat in hand. Aidan leaned closer, studying Dexter's movements as he demonstrated a few cricket shots.

'Looks like he knows his way around a bat,' Bill commented.

Aidan nodded absently, his focus entirely on the

screen. He watched as Dexter handed the bat back to Elijah and, a little later, gathered his things to leave.

'What time is this?' Aidan asked.

Bill squinted at the timestamp in the corner of the screen. 'Two minutes past ten. By this clock, anyway.'

Aidan jotted this down in his notebook. 'And Elijah?'

They continued watching as Elijah remained at the table, finishing his drink. Just over two minutes later, he stood and left the pub, cricket bag in hand.

'Okay, can we go to the car park now?'

'What for?' Bill asked. 'It's raining.'

'Oh. No, I don't mean… I mean can you bring up the car park CCTV from Saturday night.'

'Problem there,' Bill replied, pursing his lips. 'The outside CCTV don't work. Someone, mentioning no names,' he said, pointing theatrically to himself, 'might have accidentally ordered indoor cameras instead of the waterproof outdoor ones a few months back. Three days, those lasted. I've been meaning to get up there and fit new ones, but…'

'I understand. That's all I need,' Aidan said, straightening up. 'Thank you, Bill. This has been very helpful. I'll need to take a backup, if that's okay?'

As they made their way back downstairs, Aidan's mind was racing. The timeline was tight, but it was possible. Elijah could have staged the attack after Dexter left.

Back in the bar, Aidan shook Bill's hand. 'Thanks again for your help. If you remember anything else, please give me a call.' He handed Bill his card.

'Will do,' Bill nodded. 'Good luck with your investigation.'

Aidan headed for the door, his determination renewed. As he climbed into his car, his phone buzzed. A text from Sara.

> Where are you? Caroline's looking for you.

Aidan's thumb hovered over the keypad, a familiar tightness in his chest. He pictured Sara at her desk, probably leaning over to check Elijah's computer screen, their heads close together. He pushed the image away, focusing on the task at hand.

> Following a lead. Tell Caroline I'll update her soon.

He started the engine, decision made. He'd follow this lead, wherever it took him. For Dexter's sake, and for the integrity of the force.

As he pulled away from the Three Crowns, Aidan couldn't shake the feeling that he was missing something crucial.

33

The atmosphere was thick as Caroline's car bumped along the gravel track leading into Burley Wood. She pulled up behind the cordon of police vehicles, their blue lights casting an eerie glow through the trees. The air was crisp and damp, carrying the earthy scent of decaying leaves and wet soil.

Caroline took a deep breath, steeling herself for what lay ahead. She glanced at Elijah in the passenger seat, noting his composed demeanour. 'Ready?' she asked.

Elijah nodded, his face a mask of professional determination. 'Yes, boss.'

They stepped out of the car, the gravel crunching under their feet. Caroline zipped up her jacket against the chill, while Elijah straightened his tie. They made their way towards the crime scene, ducking under the blue and white police tape that fluttered in the breeze.

A young PC greeted them, his breath visible in the

cold morning air. 'Morning, ma'am, sir,' he said, nodding respectfully. 'PC Paul Wardle. The body's just through there.' He pointed towards a thicket of dense undergrowth about fifty meters away.

Caroline nodded. 'What can you tell us?'

PC Wardle consulted his notebook. 'Dog walker found her about an hour ago. Female, early-to-mid-twenties by the looks of it. No ID on the body. The dog apparently started barking and wouldn't leave the area. That's when the walker investigated and found... well, you know.'

'Right, thanks,' Caroline said. She turned to Elijah. 'Shall we?'

As they began to move towards the undergrowth, Elijah spoke up. 'Boss, if you don't mind, I'd like to take a look at the surrounding area first. Might give us some context before we see the body.'

Caroline raised an eyebrow, impressed by his methodical approach. 'Good thinking. Lead on.'

Elijah moved carefully around the perimeter of the scene, his eyes scanning the ground. The rest of the investigative team watched curiously as Elijah took charge, with the DI following close behind.

'Look here,' he said, pointing to a set of marks in the soft earth. 'Drag marks. Looks like the body was pulled into the undergrowth.'

Caroline knelt down for a closer look, the damp soaking into the knees of her trousers. The marks were clear - two parallel lines leading into the thicket. 'Good spot. What else?'

Elijah continued his circuit, pausing every few steps to examine something. His thoroughness was admirable, Caroline thought. He was leaving no stone unturned.

'Tyre tracks over there,' he said, gesturing to a patch of muddy ground near where they had parked. 'Looks fresh. Could be our killer's vehicle.'

'Or could be one of ours,' Caroline cautioned, always mindful of not jumping to conclusions.

'True,' Elijah nodded, accepting the correction gracefully. 'But worth noting all the same. We can check it against the treads of the police vehicles later.'

As they completed their circle, Elijah stopped short. 'Boss, look at this.' He pointed to a small, disturbed area just on the edge of the undergrowth. The leaves were scuffed away, revealing bare earth beneath. 'The ground here is more heavily trampled. This could be where...' He trailed off, his implication clear.

Caroline nodded grimly. 'Where she was killed. Good work, Elijah. Let's take a look at the body.'

They made their way carefully through the undergrowth, mindful not to disturb any potential evidence. The branches caught at their clothes, and the smell of damp vegetation was overwhelming. As they pushed through the last of the bushes, they finally saw her.

The body lay crumpled on the ground, partially obscured by fallen leaves. Her limbs were bent at unnatural angles, and her skin had taken on a waxy, pale hue. Caroline felt her stomach tighten at the sight, a familiar mix of sadness and determination washing over her, which soon gave way to a jolt of adrenaline as her eyes fell on the young woman's facial features. Despite her condition, there was no mistaking her identity.

'It's Sophie Trent,' she said quietly, aside to Elijah.

'Shit.'

Caroline's head whirled with a thousand and one thoughts. 'Yeah. Shit.'

Elijah knelt down, his eyes roving over the scene. His face remained professional, but Caroline could see the tightness around his eyes, the only sign of the emotion he was suppressing.

'Blunt force trauma to the head,' he said quietly, pointing to the visible injuries on her face. 'Multiple impacts, by the looks of it. And some bruising to the neck. Possible strangulation?'

Caroline nodded, impressed again by his attention to detail. 'Looks that way. We'll need to wait for the post-mortem to confirm, of course.'

'Of course,' Elijah agreed. He stood up, carefully brushing leaves from his trousers. 'What do you think, boss? Killed elsewhere and dumped here?'

Caroline considered for a moment, her eyes scanning the scene. 'Possible. The drag marks suggest she was at least moved once she was here. But that disturbed area you pointed out... she might have been finished off here.'

Elijah nodded thoughtfully. 'Either way, the killer must have had a vehicle. It's too far to carry a body from any nearby roads or houses.'

'Agreed,' Caroline said. She turned to the nearest

forensic technician, a woman in her forties who was carefully photographing the area around the body. 'Make sure you get plenty of shots of those tyre tracks and the disturbed area just outside the undergrowth.'

The technician nodded, already moving to comply. 'Will do.'

As they made their way back to the inner cordon, Caroline turned to Elijah. 'Good work there. You've got a keen eye.'

Elijah smiled modestly. 'Thank you, boss. Just doing my job.'

Caroline nodded, feeling a surge of appreciation for Elijah. Despite the grim circumstances, she couldn't help but feel they were making progress. With Elijah's help, they might just crack this case yet.

'Right,' she said, addressing the assembled officers. 'I want a thorough search of the entire area. Every inch of this wood needs to be combed. Look for anything out of place – discarded items, more evidence of vehicle activity, anything.'

The officers nodded, breaking off into teams to begin the search. Caroline turned back to Elijah. 'We need to have her identity confirmed as soon as possible. In the meantime, we need to work on the assumption it is Sophie Trent.'

'I think you're right,' Elijah replied. 'That's her.'

Caroline's phone buzzed in her pocket. She pulled it out, frowning at the screen. 'It's Sara. Apparently Aidan's following a lead and will update me soon.'

Elijah raised an eyebrow. 'Bit mysterious, isn't it?'

Caroline nodded, a hint of concern crossing her face. 'Yes, it is. I'll have a word with him when we get back.'

Both detectives watched the specialists at work in front of them, lost in thought, their minds racing from the grim discovery in Burley Wood.

34

Dexter stared at the article on his phone, his hands trembling. The garish headline glared back at him:

COPPER CLOBBERS COLLEAGUE: RUTLAND POLICE DESCEND INTO CHAOS.

He sat motionless on his worn sofa, the chill of the morning seeping through his thin t-shirt. But he barely noticed the cold. His eyes were fixed on the article, each word feeling like a physical blow. Phrases jumped out at him: 'violent assault', 'internal strife', 'questions of competence'. His stomach churned as he read Leah MacGregor's vivid description of his alleged attack on Elijah.

The impossibility of the situation overwhelmed him. He read the article again, then a third time, searching for any hint of doubt, any suggestion that this might all be a misunderstanding. But there was none.

His gaze fell on his mobile, sitting innocently on the coffee table. Before he could second-guess himself, he snatched it up and dialled Caroline's number.

She answered on the third ring. 'Dex?'

'Have you seen it?' he asked, his voice tight with barely contained emotion.

There was a pause, then a sigh. 'Yes, I've seen it.'

'It's all lies,' Dexter said, the words tumbling out in a rush. 'You know I'd never—'

'Dex,' Caroline cut in, her tone careful, 'you know I can't discuss this with you.'

He felt a surge of frustration. 'But Caroline, they're dragging my name through the mud. My whole career—'

'I know,' she said, and he could hear the genuine regret in her voice. 'But you're suspended, Dex. I can't involve you in any aspect of this case.'

Dexter closed his eyes, fighting back the wave of despair threatening to engulf him. 'What am I supposed to do? Just sit here while my life falls apart?'

There was another pause, longer this time. When Caroline spoke again, her voice was softer. 'I'm doing everything I can, Dex. You have to trust me.'

He wanted to believe her. God, how he wanted to. But the weight of the accusations, the uncertainty of his future, it all felt overwhelming. The silence in his flat seemed to press in on him, emphasising how alone he truly was.

'I don't know if I can,' he admitted, hating how vulnerable he sounded.

'Dexter—' Caroline started, but he cut her off.

'No, I get it. You can't discuss the case. Just... just tell me there's hope, boss. Tell me this isn't the end.'

The silence stretched between them, heavy with unspoken words and shared history. Dexter could almost see Caroline's furrowed brow, the way she always looked when wrestling with a difficult decision.

'It's not the end,' Caroline said finally. 'But Dex, you need to stay away. Don't contact anyone on the team. Don't try to investigate on your own. Promise me.'

Dexter's grip tightened on the phone. Every instinct screamed at him to fight, to prove his innocence. But he knew Caroline was right. Any misstep now could be fatal to his career.

'I promise,' he said, the words tasting bitter in his mouth.

'Good,' Caroline replied, relief evident in her voice. 'Take care of yourself, Dex. I'll be in touch when I can.'

The line went dead, leaving Dexter alone with the echoes of their conversation and the article back on the screen before him.

He looked around his flat, at the sparse furnishings and the walls bare of any personal touches. His whole life had been his job. Without it, who was he? The question echoed in his mind, bringing with it a flood of memories.

He thought of his first day on the force, the pride he'd felt putting on the uniform. He remembered late nights poring over case files, the rush of adrenaline during arrests, the satisfaction of bringing criminals to justice. All of it now felt like it belonged to someone else, a stranger whose life he'd been living.

Dexter's gaze drifted to the framed photo on his bookshelf, a group shot from his passing out ceremony. For a moment, a dark thought flitted through his mind, echoing a night years ago he'd tried hard to forget. The depths of despair he'd felt then, the moment of hesitation that had saved his life.

He shook his head violently, dispelling the memory. No, he wouldn't go down that road again. He had to believe in Caroline, in the team. They would clear his name. They had to.

Dexter reached for his laptop. If he couldn't investigate the case, he could at least start preparing his defence. He opened a new document and began typing, detailing his version of events, his history with Elijah, anything that might help exonerate him.

As he worked, Dexter felt a spark of the old determination returning. He might be down, but he wasn't out. Not yet. He'd weather this storm, just as he had every other challenge in his life.

Hours passed as Dexter worked, the silence of his flat broken only by the clacking of keys. When he finally looked up, the sun was setting, casting long shadows across the room. He rubbed his eyes, feeling the strain of staring at the screen for so long.

His phone buzzed with a text. For a moment, hope

flared in his chest. But it was just a generic message from his service provider. No word from Caroline, no miraculous resolution to his predicament.

Dexter sighed, closing his laptop. The work had been a good distraction, but reality was creeping back in. He stood, stretching out the kinks in his back, and walked to the window.

Outside, life went on. People hurried home from work, couples strolled hand in hand, a group of kids kicked a football around. It all seemed so normal, so infuriatingly ordinary.

He pressed his forehead against the cool glass, closing his eyes. Tomorrow would be another day of waiting, of hoping for news, of fighting against the despair that threatened to overwhelm him.

But he would face it. He had to. Because somewhere out there, the truth was waiting to be uncovered. And Dexter Antoine was nothing if not persistent.

With one last look at the world outside, he turned away from the window. One day at a time, he reminded himself silently. That's all he could do for now. One day at a time.

35

Aidan hunched over his desk, eyes fixed on the dual monitors before him. On one screen, the CCTV footage from the Three Crowns played out. He'd been at it for hours, cross-referencing timestamps and scrutinising every frame.

His coffee had long since gone cold, forgotten in the intensity of his focus. The office around him was quiet, most of his colleagues out, speaking to people in connection with the murder at Burley Wood. Aidan knew he should be helping with that, but he couldn't shake the feeling that this was important too. That somewhere in these endless loops of footage lay the key to exonerating Dexter.

He rubbed his tired eyes, forcing himself to concentrate. Something wasn't quite right, but he couldn't put his finger on it. He played the pub footage again, watching as Dexter left shortly after ten o'clock. He must have watched it dozens of times already, but this time he spotted something he hadn't noticed before.

Aidan leaned in closer, squinting at the screen. It would have been easy to have missed it, or to see it as completely insignificant, but the bolt of adrenaline in his chest confirmed his suspicions.

Through the window at the front of the pub, beyond where Dexter and Elijah had been sitting, the brake lights of a car illuminated as the vehicle reached the end of the pub's driveway, before flickering off a moment before the car turned out onto the road. The shape of the brake lights was unmistakeable: four bright red rounded squares, with four smaller ones at the edge. Even from this distance, and through the pub's window, it was so distinctive and so clearly a Land Rover Defender – the same car Dexter drove.

Aidan wound back a few frames. In the split-second between the blinding brake lights going out and the car turning left, a partial numberplate was visible. It wasn't complete, but it was undoubtedly Dexter's car.

He noted the timestamp from the CCTV system and flicked over to main camera in the bar, winding back to find the exact moment Elijah left the Three Crowns. It was then that it occurred to him. Elijah was walking home. Why had he left through the back door, towards the car park?

Before he could come up with an answer, Aidan found the exact frame where Elijah stepped outside the pub. He looked at the timestamp. Elijah stepped outside the pub exactly nine seconds before Dexter's car pulled out onto the road. Aidan reckoned it probably took about that long, if not more, to get from the car park to the road in the first place.

Nine seconds certainly wasn't enough time for Elijah to walk across the car park, have Dexter approach him and say the things he was supposed to have said, grabbed his cricket bat, beaten him up with it, got in his car, started it up, manoeuvred out of his parking space and driven down to the end of the driveway. No chance.

'Got you,' Aidan whispered, scribbling notes furiously. This was it – proof that Dexter couldn't possibly have attacked Elijah.

He sat back in his chair, mind racing. If it wasn't Dexter, who was it? And why would Elijah say it was him? He even claimed they'd had a conversation. Why would he go to such lengths to frame Dexter? The implications were staggering. If Dexter was innocent, it meant the real attacker was still out there. And it meant Elijah Drummond was clever enough and evil enough to stage this elaborate deception.

Aidan reached for his phone, then hesitated. He should tell Caroline about this immediately. But a small voice in the back of his mind held him back. What if he was wrong? What if he was seeing patterns that weren't there, driven by his desire to clear Dexter's name?

No, he decided. He needed to be sure. He'd go over the footage again, document everything meticulously. Build an ironclad case before presenting it to Caroline.

Aidan's fingers flew across the keyboard, documenting every single thing he'd found. The click-clack of keys filled the empty office, a staccato rhythm that matched his racing thoughts. He was vaguely aware of the sun setting outside, casting long shadows across his desk, but he paid it no mind.

Time seemed to stretch and compress, minutes blurring into hours as he pored over the footage again and again. Each viewing revealed new details, small inconsistencies that built up into a compelling case.

It wasn't until his stomach growled loudly that Aidan finally looked up from his screens. He blinked, disoriented, and fumbled for his phone, checking the time.

Christ. He'd been at it for over two hours straight.

Aidan leaned back in his chair, his neck and shoulders protesting the movement. His eyes felt gritty, and a dull headache pulsed behind his temples. But none of that mattered.

Because there, laid out in meticulous detail on the notepad beside him, was the fruit of his labour. Not just a hunch or a theory, but solid, documented evidence.

Evidence that might just save an innocent man.

The implications sent a chill down his spine. Suddenly, the quiet, empty office felt a lot less safe.

36

The damp chill of Burley Wood had settled into Caroline's bones. She stamped her feet, trying to generate some warmth as she continued to watch the forensics team meticulously comb through the undergrowth. Elijah stood nearby, his brow furrowed in concentration as he made notes in a small, leather-bound notebook.

A shrill ring cut through the air, startling a nearby blackbird into frantic flight. Caroline fumbled in her pocket, pulling out her mobile. Aidan's name flashed on the screen.

'Aidan,' she answered, turning slightly away from Elijah. 'What is it?'

Aidan's voice crackled through the speaker, barely audible. '...found something... Dexter... CCTV footage...'

Caroline frowned, pressing the phone harder against her ear. 'Aidan, I can barely hear you. The signal out here is awful. Can't this wait until I'm back at the station?'

But Aidan was insistent, his words tumbling out in a rush of static and excitement. Caroline caught fragments – 'car park', 'brake lights', 'nine seconds' – but the details were lost in the poor connection.

'Aidan, slow down,' she said, trying to keep the frustration out of her voice. 'I can't—'

She broke off as she caught Elijah watching her, his expression curious. Caroline turned away again, lowering her voice. 'Look, I'm still at the scene. I'll call you back when—'

Aidan's voice suddenly came through clearly, his words stopping Caroline mid-sentence. Her eyes widened slightly, but she quickly schooled her features into neutrality.

'Are you certain?' she asked, keeping her tone level.

More crackling, then Aidan's emphatic response. Caroline listened intently, her free hand clenching and unclenching at her side.

'Right,' she said finally. 'Don't do anything else until I get back. And Aidan? Good work.'

She ended the call, slipping the phone back into her pocket. Her mind raced with the implications of what Aidan had told her, but she forced herself to take a deep breath before turning back to face Elijah.

'Everything alright?' Elijah asked, his pen poised over his notebook.

Caroline nodded, her face a mask of professional calm. 'Fine. Just Aidan updating me on some case details.'

Elijah's eyebrow raised slightly. 'Anything pertinent to our investigation here?'

For a moment, Caroline was tempted to share Aidan's findings. But caution won out. Until she could verify the information herself, it was best to keep it under wraps.

'Nothing concrete yet,' she said, managing a small smile. 'You know how it is with ongoing investigations. Lots of leads to follow up on.'

Elijah nodded, seemingly satisfied with her answer. 'Of course, boss.'

37

Caroline's hands gripped the steering wheel tightly as she pulled up outside the Trent family home. The quaint semi-detached house, with its neatly trimmed hedge and cheerful flowerbeds, seemed at odds with the grim task that lay ahead.

She took a deep breath, steeling herself. No matter how many times she'd done this, facing a recently bereaved family never got any easier.

As she walked up the path, the front door opened. A woman in her early fifties stood there, hope and fear warring in her eyes. 'Detective Inspector Hills?'

Caroline nodded. 'Mrs Trent? May I come in?'

Once inside, Caroline found herself sitting across from Sophie's parents, Andrew and Pamela Trent, in their cosy living room. Family photos adorned the walls, Sophie's smiling face a painful reminder of why she was here.

Pamela's anguished cry broke the silence. Andrew

wrapped an arm around his wife, his own face a mask of shock and grief.

Caroline gave them a moment, her heart heavy. When the initial wave of grief had subsided, she spoke again. 'I know this is incredibly difficult, but I need to ask you some questions. It could help us find out what happened to Sophie.'

Pamela nodded, wiping her eyes. 'Of course. Anything to help.'

'Did Sophie have any enemies? Anyone who might have wanted to harm her?'

Andrew shook his head. 'No, everyone loved Sophie. She was... she was such a kind soul.'

'What about relationships? Was she seeing anyone currently or had any difficult breakups recently?'

Pamela sniffled. 'She'd been single for a while. Her last relationship ended about six months ago, but it was amicable. They're still friends on Facebook.'

Caroline made a mental note to follow up on that. 'And her connection to Emily Ashcroft? Do you know if anyone might have had a reason to want both of them dead?'

Andrew and Pamela exchanged a bewildered look. 'We... we didn't even think their deaths might be connected.'

Caroline chose her words carefully. 'We're exploring all possibilities at this stage.'

She paused, then asked, 'Do you know what Sophie was doing in Burley Wood?'

Pamela's brow furrowed. 'She said she was going to visit a friend.'

'Did you see her leave?'

Pamela nodded. 'Yes, she went up to her room to get a jacket. Just before she left, I saw her send a message on her phone. It said, "Just leaving now". I assume it was to her friend.'

Caroline leaned forward slightly. 'Which friend was she going to see?'

Pamela thought for a moment. 'You know, I didn't actually ask. Oh god. I should have, shouldn't I?'

'You can't blame yourself,' Caroline said, jotting down notes. 'Sophie was a grown adult. What time was this?'

'I'm not sure. Late morning, I think it was.'

Caroline's mind raced with the implications. 'Was Sophie particularly security conscious about her devices?'

Andrew and Pamela exchanged a glance. 'It started a couple of months ago,' Andrew said. 'She became very interested in online privacy. Started using encrypted messaging apps, that sort of thing.'

'Did she ever explain why?'

Pamela shook her head. 'Not really. She just said it was important to be careful these days.'

Caroline kept her face neutral, but internally, alarm bells were ringing.

Caroline was up in Sophie's bedroom when her phone rang. Aidan's name flashed on the screen.

'Aidan,' she answered, 'what have you got?'

'Boss, we've accessed Sophie's phone,' Aidan's voice came through. 'You won't believe this – her PIN was just her date of birth.'

Caroline frowned. 'That doesn't sound like someone who's security conscious. What did you find?'

'That's just it,' Aidan replied, his voice tense. 'There's no message saying "Just leaving now". In fact, there are no recent messages to or from anyone.'

Caroline's pulse quickened. 'Are you certain?'

'Positive. I've gone through it twice. Something's not adding up here.'

Caroline's eyes scanned the room, landing on Sophie's iPad on the bedside table. 'Aidan, what was that PIN again?'

Aidan recited the numbers, and Caroline picked up the iPad. She noticed it was in flight mode, a detail that hadn't come up in her conversation with the Trents.

She entered the PIN, and the iPad unlocked immediately. 'I'm in,' she said, opening the Messages app.

'Boss?' Aidan's voice crackled through the speaker.

'Hold on, Aidan,' Caroline muttered, her eyes widening as she scrolled through the messages. 'There's a whole conversation here with someone, including the "Just leaving now" message Mrs Trent mentioned. It was sent at 11:23 AM.'

'What?' Aidan's surprise was evident. 'But there's nothing like that on her phone. How is that possible?'

Caroline looked more closely at the screen. 'It's in flight mode,' she said.

'Someone must have deleted the messages from her phone, and because her iPad's offline the deletion hasn't synced.'

Caroline continued scrolling through the messages. 'The contact is saved as "Bestie", followed by a heart emoji.'

'Can you see the number?' Aidan asked

'Yes, I've got it,' Caroline said, reading out the number. 'Aidan, I need you to trace this number's owner immediately. And keep me on the line while you do it.'

'On it, boss,' Aidan replied. Caroline could hear him typing furiously in the background.

While she waited, Caroline carefully placed the iPad into an evidence bag, sealing it. She'd need to get this back to the station for a thorough examination by the tech team.

'Boss,' Aidan's voice came back, sounding confused. 'I've got a hit on that number.'

'Go on,' Caroline urged, her heart racing.

'It's registered to Lucy Palmer.'

39

Caroline's fingers hovered over her phone, her mind racing. She knew she needed someone she could trust implicitly to help her navigate this increasingly complex case.

She couldn't turn to Elijah, not after Aidan's discoveries about his deception. Sara was compromised by her involvement with Elijah, and Aidan was too caught up in the internal drama to be of much use right now. There was only one person she could rely on, suspended or not.

Taking a deep breath, she dialled Dexter's number.

He answered on the second ring, his voice cautious. 'Boss?'

'Dex, I need you,' she said without preamble.

'How do you mean?'

'I need you to meet me. There's been a murder, and the IP is a friend of Emily Ashcroft's.'

Dexter sighed. 'I'm suspended, in case you hadn't noticed.'

'I know you are, but I don't care. I need you with me on this case.'

There was a pause, then Dexter's voice came back, hesitant. 'Boss, I appreciate the vote of confidence, but you know I can't—'

'Forget the suspension,' Caroline interrupted, her tone brooking no argument. 'I'll deal with the fallout later. I know for a fact you're innocent, Dex. And right now, I need your mind on this case more than I need to follow protocol. Honestly, just trust me on this. I'll take the flak. If anyone asks, I told you your suspension was lifted.'

Another pause, longer this time. Caroline could almost hear the gears turning in Dexter's head.

'Where are you?' he asked finally.

'I'm just leaving the IP's house,' Caroline replied, relief washing over her. 'Can you meet me in the Burley Road car park in half an hour?'

'If I leave now and floor it,' Dexter said, a new determination in his voice.

Caroline ended the call and quickly gathered her things. She made her apologies to the Trents, explaining that she needed to follow up on an urgent lead. As she left the house, she felt a renewed sense of purpose. With Dexter by her side, she was confident they could unravel this mystery.

. . .

Thirty minutes later, Caroline pulled up in the car park. Dexter was already there, leaning against his car. As she got out, she saw the mixture of emotions playing across his face – relief, gratitude, and a hint of apprehension.

'Thanks for coming, Dex,' she said, walking over to him.

Dexter nodded, straightening up. 'Of course. But look, are you sure about this? If anyone finds out—'

'Let me worry about that,' Caroline cut him off. 'Right now, we've got bigger problems to deal with.'

Caroline quickly filled him in on what she'd discovered at the Trent house, and the discrepancies between Sophie's phone and iPad. As she spoke, she could see Dexter's investigative instincts kicking in, his eyes lighting up with the thrill of piecing together a puzzle.

'So what's our next move?' Dexter asked as she finished.

'We need to talk to Lucy,' Caroline said. 'But we need to tread carefully. We don't want to spook her if she is involved, but we also can't ignore the possibility that she might be in danger too. If this is linked with the whistleblowing at EWMS, Lucy could be in danger too – especially if Emily or Sophie confided in her.'

Dexter nodded, already moving towards Caroline's car. 'Then let's not waste any more time. Where does she live?'

As they got into the car, Caroline felt a sense of rightness settle over her. This was how it should be – she and Dexter, working together to solve the case. Whatever consequences came from her decision to bring him in, she knew it was the right call.

'Ready?' she asked, starting the engine.

Dexter gave her a small smile. 'Always.'

40

Caroline's car pulled up outside Lucy Palmer's house, a modest semi-detached property on a quiet street in Langham. The curtains were drawn, and there was no sign of movement inside. The late afternoon sun cast long shadows across the neatly trimmed front lawn.

'Doesn't look like anyone's home,' Dexter remarked, peering through the windscreen.

'Let's find out,' Caroline replied, unbuckling her seatbelt. 'Remember, we're treading carefully here.'

Dexter nodded, his face serious. 'Agreed.'

They approached the front door, both acutely aware of the delicate nature of their visit. Caroline rang the doorbell, and they waited, listening for any sounds of movement within.

After a moment, they heard footsteps, and the door opened to reveal Lucy Palmer. She looked tired, her eyes red-rimmed as if she'd been crying. Her dark hair was pulled back in a messy ponytail, and she wore a baggy jumper that seemed to swallow her small frame.

'Hi Lucy,' Caroline said, smiling. 'We'd like to ask you a few questions about Sophie Trent, if that's alright.'

Lucy's eyes widened slightly at the mention of Sophie's name, a flash of something – fear? grief? – crossing her face. 'Oh, um, of course,' she said, her voice barely above a whisper. 'Has something happened to her?'

Caroline and Dexter exchanged a quick glance. 'Perhaps we could come in and talk?' Caroline suggested gently.

Lucy hesitated for a moment, then nodded. 'Yes, sorry. Please, come in.' She stepped back, allowing them into the house.

They followed Lucy into a small living room, tastefully decorated but with a lived-in feel. Photos adorned the walls, and a half-empty mug of tea sat on the coffee table. Lucy perched on the edge of an armchair, while Caroline and Dexter took seats on the sofa opposite.

'Lucy,' Caroline began, her tone gentle but firm, 'I'm afraid we have some difficult news. Sophie's body was found earlier today.'

Lucy's face crumpled, her hand flying to her mouth. 'No,' she whispered, tears welling in her eyes. 'No, that can't be right. I just spoke to her... we had lunch...'

Dexter leaned forward, his voice soft. 'We're very sorry for your loss, Lucy. We understand you were close friends.'

Lucy nodded, wiping at her eyes. 'We've known each other since uni. She's... she was a good friend.'

Caroline gave Lucy a moment to compose herself before continuing. 'We're trying to piece together Sophie's movements on the day she disappeared. Can you tell us when you last saw or spoke to her?'

Lucy took a shaky breath. 'I saw her the day before yesterday. We had lunch together in Oakham. At that little café in the castle, you know?'

'And did you speak to her after that?' Dexter asked, his tone carefully neutral.

Lucy shook her head. 'No, I... I tried calling her yesterday, but she didn't answer. I just thought she was busy with work or something. I never thought...' She trailed off, fresh tears spilling down her cheeks.

Caroline and Dexter exchanged another quick glance. 'Would you mind if we took a look at your phone?' Caroline asked. 'Just to confirm any communications between you and Sophie?'

Lucy hesitated for a moment, then nodded. 'Of course,' she said, reaching for her phone on the coffee table. She unlocked it and handed it to Caroline. 'I've got nothing to hide.'

As Caroline scrolled through Lucy's messages, Dexter's gaze wandered around the room. His eyes swept over the family photos on the walls, the books on the shelves, looking for anything that might give them more insight into Lucy's life – and her connection to Sophie.

'Have you always lived in this house?' he asked, keeping his tone conversational.

Lucy looked up, seeming grateful for the distraction. 'I moved here just before my third birthday.'

'And Sophie?' Dexter pressed gently. 'Did she come here often?'

Lucy nodded. 'Yeah, sometimes.'

Lucy's phone buzzed in Caroline's hand. Lucy glanced at it, then stood up. 'I'm sorry, would you mind if I just got myself a glass of water? My throat's a bit dry.'

'Of course,' Caroline said, handing the phone back. 'Take your time.'

As Lucy left the room, Caroline and Dexter exchanged a glance. Caroline's eyes then drifted to a framed photograph on the sideboard. She stood up, moving closer to get a better look.

'Wait,' she said, her voice barely above a whisper. 'Isn't that...'

Dexter joined her, studying the photo. His eyes widened in recognition.

41

'That's Kevin Hartley, isn't it?' Dexter said.

'That's what I thought. Why would she have a framed photo of him? Look. He's in others, too,' Caroline replied, not noticing that Dexter had stepped into the kitchen. 'I'm guessing this must be his wife next to him.'

'Karen,' Dexter said, re-entering the room. He held an envelope in front of Caroline. 'Just found this on the side. Kevin and Karen Hartley. KH and KH.'

Caroline nodded slowly, the implications of this discovery sinking in. 'Emily wasn't having secret liaisons with Kevin Hartley at all. It was his wife, Karen. But how does Lucy... Oh shit.'

Caroline's eyes rested on another photograph.

'Boss?' Dexter asked. 'What is it?'

Caroline picked up the photo. In it, Kevin and Karen had their arms around a much younger – yet unmistakeable – Lucy.

'The Hartleys are Lucy's adoptive parents,' she said.

'So if Lucy had discovered the affair...' Dexter trailed off, the implications hanging heavy in the air.

'It would have shattered her world,' Caroline said. 'Emily would have become the villain in her eyes, the one who corrupted her perfect mother.'

Dexter leaned back, running a hand over his face. 'And Sophie? Where does she fit into all this?'

Just as the full weight of their realisation settled over them, a sound from outside caught their attention. The unmistakable roar of a car engine starting up, followed by the screech of tyres on the road.

Caroline and Dexter locked eyes for a split second before rushing to the window. They were just in time to see Lucy's car speeding away, already halfway down the street.

'Shit!' Caroline shouted. 'Go. Go!'

Dexter was already moving towards the door.

As they burst out of the house, Lucy's car was disappearing around the corner at the end of the street.

Caroline fumbled for her car keys. 'Call it in,' she ordered Dexter. 'We need to find her before she does something drastic.'

They raced to Caroline's car, the gravity of the situation settling over them. Lucy Palmer, the quiet, unassuming young woman, was now their main suspect. And she was on the run.

42

Caroline gunned the engine as they peeled away from Lucy's house, tyres screeching in protest. Dexter gripped the door handle, his eyes scanning the road ahead.

'Which way?' Caroline barked, approaching the end of the street.

'Right,' Dexter said decisively. 'It takes you out to the main road. She's got to have gone that way.'

Caroline swung the car right, the centrifugal force pressing them into their seats. The quiet streets blurred past as they sped along, searching for any sign of Lucy's car.

'Don't let them fob you off,' Caroline ordered, her eyes never leaving the road. 'We need all available units on this.'

Dexter nodded, speaking firmly into his phone. 'Control, this is DS Antoine. We're in pursuit of a suspect in the Sophie Trent murder case. Suspect is Lucy Palmer, driving a...' He paused, realising he didn't know the make of Lucy's car.

'Red Corsa,' Caroline supplied, remembering the fleeting glimpse they'd caught as Lucy sped away.

'...a red Vauxhall Corsa,' Dexter continued. 'We don't have the registration. You'll need to check the PNC for vehicles registered to Lucy Palmer.'

'Understood,' came the reply. 'We'll get units heading your way. What's your current location?'

Dexter relayed their position between Langham and Burley as Caroline navigated the winding roads, her focus intense.

'There!' Dexter suddenly exclaimed, pointing ahead. In the distance, they could just make out a red car disappearing around a bend.

Caroline pressed her foot down harder on the accelerator. The gap between them and Lucy's car slowly began to close.

'I can almost make out the plate,' Dexter said, leaning forward in his seat and squinting. 'It's... Lima... Delta... Two...'

But Caroline wasn't listening. Her eyes had locked onto something ahead - something that made her blood run cold.

'Dex,' she said, her voice tense. 'The level crossing.'

Up ahead, the barriers of a railway crossing were lowering, red lights flashing in warning. And beyond that, Caroline could see the approaching train, its horn blaring in the distance.

Lucy's car showed no signs of slowing down.

'She's not stopping,' Dexter said, his voice filled with disbelief.

Caroline gripped the steering wheel tighter, her knuckles white. 'Come on, Lucy,' she muttered. 'Don't do this.'

But Lucy's car continued to barrel towards the crossing, seeming to pick up speed rather than slow down.

The train's horn blared louder, the sound filling the air as it hurtled towards the intersection. Caroline and Dexter watched in horror as Lucy's car reached the barriers.

There was a sickening crunch of metal as the Corsa smashed through the lowered barrier. For a heart-stopping moment, it looked like the car would clear the tracks.

Then the train was upon them, its massive form filling their view. Caroline slammed on the brakes, bringing their car to a screeching halt just short of the crossing.

A cacophony of sounds filled the air, drowning out everything else. Caroline and Dexter could only watch, helpless, as the train hurtled towards Lucy's car.

43

The world seemed to move in slow motion as Lucy's car smashed through the barrier with a sickening crunch, followed by the deafening blare of the train's horn. Caroline and Dexter watched in horror.

The train's brakes screeched, sparks flying from the wheels as it fought against its own momentum. But it was clear it wouldn't stop in time.

The rush of air from the passing train rocked their car, the noise deafening even from inside the vehicle. Caroline's heart pounded in her chest, the adrenaline surge making her feel light-headed. She tried to process what she'd just seen, her police training kicking in to keep her focused despite the shock.

Beside her, Dexter let out a shaky breath. 'Did she...?' he began, unable to finish the sentence.

As the train continued its unstoppable journey past them, horn still blaring, Caroline and Dexter strained to see beyond it. They had been so certain the car would be hit, that they'd witness the devastating impact.

But as the last carriage cleared the crossing and the dust began to settle, there was no wreckage. No twisted metal, no shattered glass. Just empty tracks and the broken barriers.

'Where is she?' Caroline muttered, her eyes scanning the area. The silence after the train's passing felt oppressive, broken only by the distant echo of the horn as it continued down the track.

Dexter pointed to the road beyond the crossing. 'Look!'

Clear skid marks marred the asphalt on the other side of the tracks, where Lucy had struggled to maintain control of the car, yet somehow managed to avoid what should have been a fatal collision.

Caroline felt a mix of relief and frustration wash over her. Relief that they hadn't just witnessed a death, but frustration that their suspect was still at large.

Before they could fully process this miraculous escape, a new sound reached their ears – a car horn blaring in the distance, accompanied by the screech of tyres.

'She's still going,' Dexter said, his voice a mix of disbelief and admiration.

Caroline didn't waste another second. She manoeuvred their car around the lowered barrier, careful to avoid the debris from Lucy's reckless crossing. As they cleared the tracks, they could see the aftermath of another near-miss further down the road.

A car was pulled over on the shoulder, its driver

standing outside, gesticulating wildly. He'd clearly had to swerve to avoid Lucy's car as she'd come flying off the tracks.

Caroline slowed as they approached the shaken driver. 'Are you okay?' she called through the open window.

The driver nodded nervously.

'We'll have someone with you shortly. Don't move.'

As Dexter relayed their position to the control room, the dispatcher confirmed that backup was en route.

Ahead of them, a cloud of dust marked Lucy's continued flight. As they accelerated after her, the gravity of the situation settled over them.

Lucy Palmer was no longer just a suspect in a murder investigation. Her reckless driving had escalated the situation, putting countless lives at risk. Whatever her reasons, whatever her guilt or innocence in the original crimes, she had now crossed a line that there was no coming back from.

As fields and hedgerows flew past, Caroline's mind raced. Where was Lucy going? What was her endgame? And most importantly, how were they going to stop her before someone else got hurt?

The answers lay somewhere up ahead, beyond the next bend in the road. All they could do now was follow the trail of dust and pray they caught up before it was too late.

44

The engine roared as they picked up speed, both of them scanning the road ahead for any sign of Lucy's red Corsa.

Dexter pulled out his phone, his fingers flying over the keypad as he dialled the control room.

'This is DS Antoine,' he said, his voice tense. 'Suspect Lucy Palmer just drove through a level crossing barrier, narrowly avoiding a collision with a train. No injuries reported, but significant damage to railway property. Suspect still at large, heading east.'

As Dexter relayed the information, Caroline's eyes remained fixed on the road. The adrenaline coursing through her veins sharpened her focus, every sense on high alert.

They rounded a bend, and Caroline instinctively eased off the accelerator. Up ahead, a Nissan Micra was pulled over on the side of the road, its hazard lights flashing.

'Ignore it,' Dexter said. 'We need to gain ground.'

'Call it in,' Caroline replied, her eyes once again fixed on the road ahead. 'Someone can check on him.'

Dexter nodded, settling back into his seat. The chase was back on, and they both knew that every second counted. Somewhere up ahead, Lucy Palmer was still running. And they had to catch her before she hurt herself – or someone else.

45

At high speed, the landscape became a blur of green fields and hedgerows. Caroline's knuckles were white on the steering wheel, her eyes fixed ahead, searching for any flash of red among the greenery.

As they reached the junction with the A606 at Whitwell, they caught a glance of Lucy's car turning into Bull Brig Lane, a few yards further up.

'She's heading towards the water,' Dexter said, his voice tight with tension as Caroline swerved out onto the main road, narrowly avoiding a van. Her car's tyres squealed as she made the tight turn into Bull Brig Lane, desperate to gain ground on Lucy.

The trees thinned as they reached the boat park, revealing the vast expanse of the reservoir. Sunlight glinted off the water's surface, momentarily dazzling them.

As they drew closer, they could see Lucy's car, parked

near the slipway at the water's edge. They watched as Lucy herself emerged, her movements jerky and frantic.

Caroline eased off the accelerator, the car slowing as they approached. The low rumble of their tyres seemed deafening in the tense silence.

Lucy's head snapped towards them. For a moment, she stood frozen, like a deer in headlights. Then she dove back into her car.

Caroline brought their vehicle to a stop, leaving a cautious distance between them. She cut the engine, the sudden silence broken only by the sound of the water teasing at the slipway and the aggressive idle of Lucy's car.

Caroline's hand hovered over the door handle. She glanced at Dexter, seeing her own uncertainty mirrored in his eyes.

'Careful,' he murmured, nodding towards Lucy's car.

Caroline nodded, taking a deep breath before slowly opening her door. The creak of hinges seemed to echo across the water.

'Lucy!' she called out, her voice steady despite the adrenaline coursing through her veins. 'We need to talk about this!'

The seconds stretched, feeling like hours. Then, almost imperceptibly at first, Lucy's window began to lower.

Caroline took a tentative step forward, feeling the ground beneath her feet. She could feel Dexter moving behind her, a reassuring presence at her back.

'Lucy,' she said again, softer this time. 'Whatever's

going on, we can work this out. Just step out of the car, and we'll talk.'

The window was fully down now, but Lucy remained silent, her face partially hidden in shadow. Caroline could see her hands gripping the steering wheel tightly.

A gentle breeze rippled across the water, carrying with it the scent of algae and damp earth. A bird called in the distance, the sound jarring in the charged atmosphere.

Caroline took another step forward, her body coiled tight, ready to move at the slightest provocation. She could hear Dexter's measured breathing behind her, and knew he was poised and ready.

The moment stretched, taut as a bowstring. Caroline's every sense was on high alert – the warmth of the sun on her back, the taste of adrenaline in her mouth, the slight tremor in her outstretched hand.

Lucy shifted in her seat, and Caroline tensed. But still, Lucy made no move to flee or speak.

They were balanced on a knife's edge, and Caroline knew that the next few seconds would determine everything. One wrong move, one misspoken word, and it could all unravel.

She took a deep breath, preparing to speak again, praying she would find the right words to defuse this volatile situation.

Caroline took another cautious step forward. The gentle lapping of water against the shore filled the tense silence.

'Lucy,' she said softly, her hand outstretched. 'I know you're scared. But this isn't the way.'

Lucy's fingers tightened on the steering wheel, her knuckles white. Her eyes darted between Caroline and the water.

'You don't understand,' Lucy said, her voice barely above a whisper. 'I had no choice. They were going to ruin everything.'

Caroline's heart raced, but she kept her voice steady. 'Who, Lucy?'

'I didn't mean to do anything wrong,' Lucy said, tears welling in her eyes.

Caroline softened her voice. 'Lucy, what happened? We can help you.'

'It wasn't meant to be like this. It all just got so out of control, and… It wasn't meant to be like this. It wasn't.'

'Are you talking about Emily and Sophie?' Caroline asked.

Slowly and gently, Lucy nodded.

'But you were such good friends. And you seem like a kind, gentle person, Lucy. How on earth did it happen?'

Lucy stared vacantly towards the water, her tears subsiding as she drifted into an almost trance-like state. 'I'd had a few drinks. I took Emily to the garage for a chat in private and told her I thought Liam was cheating on her. That he was bad for her. She didn't want to hear it. She'd been drinking too and started arguing back. I'd never seen her like that. She told me to go away. Said if I wasn't going to support her choices, she didn't want me as a friend.

That's when I went to find Liam. I told him to break up with Emily. I said if he really cared for her, he'd do what was best for her. He just pushed me over and walked off. I knew I had to do something, but I didn't know what. I got up and went inside to the downstairs bathroom at the back of the house to clean myself up and sort myself out. The door's right next to the one into the garage, and I could hear Emily crying in there, so I went in. She just looked at me and told me to fuck off. There… there was a look in her eyes. I could see she was done with me. It felt like it was all over. Like he'd won. Like I'd lost her. And all I could see was his stupid, smug little face grinning at me in my mind. I don't know if I wanted to hug her or go over and shake her out of it, but as soon as I moved towards her she ran off out the side door of the garage and down the lane at the side of the house. I went after her. I still don't know why. I was just desperate. And his dirty, shit-eating grin was still right there, as if he was right in front of me. The lane goes downhill towards a little field, and it was slippy. When we were at the bottom I'd almost caught up with her, but she tripped and went over, and… and…'

'And what?' Caroline asked.

'We were on the ground in the pissing rain, just shouting at each other. I was telling her she needed to see what everyone else could see, and that Liam was going to ruin her life, but she wasn't having any of it. Then… then she said he had nothing to do with any of her choices. She said it wasn't him. It was her. And she… she told me.'

'What did she tell you, Lucy?'

'About her and Mum,' Lucy replied, her eyes turning glassy with tears. 'The way she spat it out, it was if she was proud of it. Like she'd been waiting for this moment to prove that the evil was inside her all along. It feels so crazy saying it, but something just flipped. I don't know what it was. It's like it happened, but it didn't. Like I was doing it, but I was watching someone else do it. I don't know whether it took three seconds or ten minutes, but it happened.'

'What happened?' Caroline softly asked.

'It's impossible to explain it to someone who's never felt it, but that sinking feeling you get when your whole world falls apart in an instant… I couldn't handle that. Not again. And then I was on top of her. On her back. My arm was round her neck, and my other arm was locking it in place, and I was just sort of… squeezing. Hugging. I don't know… Crushing. And then at some point she stopped. I don't know how long for. I just suddenly realised she wasn't struggling anymore. Wasn't fighting. Wasn't even there. I knew straight away what'd happened. I didn't know what to do, but I knew there was no way back. So I sort of dragged her into the long grass a bit. I don't know why. What else could I do?'

Dexter's voice came from behind Caroline, low and careful. 'And Sophie? What did she have to do with it?'

A sob escaped Lucy's throat. 'Sophie found out. About Emily and my mum. She'd come round to see me a few days ago. The day of the party. The upstairs windows were open, and when she got near the door… Don't make me say it. But that's not all...' She trailed off, her gaze distant.

'What else did Sophie know, Lucy?' Caroline prompted gently.

Lucy's eyes snapped back to Caroline, filled with a mix of fear and desperation. 'She could tell I already knew. She said she could see it on my face. And that's when she worked it out. About what happened to Emily. She was hysterical. She was going to go to the police.'

Caroline felt a chill run down her spine but pressed on. 'So you confronted her?'

'I didn't mean to,' Lucy whispered, her voice breaking. 'We argued at the top of the stairs. I just... I pushed her. I didn't think...'

'How did you move her body?' Dexter asked, his tone neutral.

'I didn't. She was still alive. She was awake, but she wasn't quite there. I apologised, told her we needed to get her to hospital, and she just sort of murmured and came with me. We got in my car and I drove off to Burley Wood. I don't know if she was concussed or... or what. When we got there, she just walked with me, sort of staring in front of her the whole time.' Lucy sobbed, fresh tears spilling down her cheeks. 'I had no choice. I panicked. I couldn't let anyone find out. So I did the same thing again. I pulled her to the ground, and locked my arm around her neck. I remember she put one of her arms up as if she was going to grab mine, but she barely even touched it. She just sort of... gave in. It's like she wasn't even there anymore.'

'Lucy,' Caroline said, taking another small step. 'I know this must have been overwhelming for you. But there are still people who care about you, who need you.'

'How?' Lucy asked, her voice cracking. 'I've destroyed everything. My family, my career... it's all gone.'

'Not if you come with us now,' Dexter interjected. 'We can help you, Lucy. But you need to step out of the car.'

A breeze ruffled Lucy's hair. For a moment, she seemed to lean towards the open window, towards Caroline's outstretched hand.

'I was so angry,' Lucy said, her voice breaking. 'Emily didn't care about anyone but herself. And Sophie... she was supposed to be my friend.'

Caroline nodded, encouraging Lucy to continue. 'I understand, Lucy. You felt betrayed, cornered.'

'They were going to destroy my family,' Lucy said, a hint of anger flashing in her eyes. 'Everything I'd worked for, gone in an instant.'

'Even when we make terrible mistakes, we can find a way to make amends. We all can.'

For a moment, Lucy seemed to consider her words. Her grip on the steering wheel loosened slightly.

Caroline's pulse quickened. Was Lucy about to give herself up?

Then, in an instant, everything changed.

Lucy's eyes hardened, her jaw set. 'I'm sorry,' she whispered. 'I can't.'

Her foot slammed down on the accelerator.

The Corsa's tyres spun on the gravel, kicking up stones. Caroline stumbled backward, Dexter's hand grabbing her arm to steady her.

They watched in horror as the car lurched forward, straight towards the water's edge.

'Lucy, no!' Caroline screamed, but it was too late.

The Corsa hit the water with a massive splash, sending waves rippling across the previously calm surface. For a moment, it bobbed there, half in and half out of the reservoir.

Then, with agonising slowness, it began to sink.

Water poured in through the open window, filling the car with frightening speed.

'We have to do something,' Dexter said, already shrugging off his jacket.

But even as he spoke, the car slipped further into the depths. The last thing they saw was Lucy's pale face, turned towards them, before the water closed over the roof of the car.

Ripples spread across the surface of the reservoir, the only evidence of the tragedy that had just unfolded.

Caroline stood frozen, her outstretched hand still reaching towards where Lucy had been moments before. The gentle lapping of waves against the shore seemed to mock the violence of what they'd just witnessed.

In the distance, a bird called, oblivious to the human drama below.

46

The water's surface rippled, the last air bubbles breaking as Lucy's car disappeared beneath the water. For a heartbeat, Caroline stood frozen, her mind struggling to process what had just happened. Lucy hadn't opened the windows to talk. She'd opened them to make sure the car sank faster.

Beside Caroline, Dexter was already in motion. He kicked off his shoes, shrugging out of his jacket.

'Call for backup!' he shouted, sprinting towards the water's edge.

Caroline was stuck to the spot, her legs filled with concrete as her eyes locked onto the lapping water, her chest tight.

She could see it all this time. Clearer than she'd ever seen it before. Things she must have forgotten, must have blocked out, but which she knew with absolute certainty were real.

It even felt the same. The sheer panic and desperation coupled with the complete inability to move a muscle or even breathe. The paralysis was overwhelming. Paralysis of body. Paralysis of rational thought. It was as if she was lost in a time loop, watching events unfold again, exactly as they had all those years ago.

One minute Stuart had been there, talking, breathing, living. And in the blink of an eye he was gone, as if he'd never even existed, whilst the relentless cycle of nature continued. The water kept moving. The grass kept swaying. The birds kept singing. And it was in those moments that the force and power of the shock became apparent. It was the sudden, enormous realisation that even though one's life and existence were everything – even though we are all the centre of our own universes – to the universe, we are nothing. It was the instantaneous and crushing acceptance that nature will swallow you whole in an instant, without a second thought and not even the merest hint of a memory. There could be no more powerful way to paralyse a human being than the abrupt revelation that everything is nothing.

'Boss! Call for backup!' Dexter yelled again, snapping her out of her trance.

Caroline fumbled for her phone, her eyes never leaving Dexter as he plunged into the reservoir. The icy water hit him like a physical blow, forcing the air from his lungs. For a moment, he floundered, the shock threatening to overwhelm him.

Then instinct kicked in. Dexter took a deep breath and dove, powerful strokes propelling him downward. The murky water stung his eyes as he searched for any sign of the sinking car.

Time seemed to stretch, each second an eternity as he pushed deeper. The pressure built in his ears, a dull ache spreading through his skull. Still, he pressed on.

The cold began to seep into his bones, his movements becoming sluggish. He kicked harder, fighting against the water's resistance. Every muscle in his body screamed for oxygen, but he forced himself to keep going.

Shapes loomed in the murky depths, teasing his vision. A log? A shadow? Each time his heart leapt, thinking he'd found the car, only to have hope fade as quickly as it had come.

His lungs burned, the urge to breathe becoming overwhelming. Dexter's mind raced, calculating how long he'd been under, how much further he could push himself. The weight of the water pressed down on him, as if trying to force the air from his chest.

Frustration mounted as he realised his body's natural buoyancy was working against him. With lungs full of air, he was fighting not just the water but his own physiology. Each downward stroke felt like swimming through treacle, his progress agonisingly slow.

Black spots danced at the edges of his vision. His body screamed at him to surface, to breathe. But the thought of

Lucy, trapped and sinking, spurred him on. Just a little further, he told himself. Just a little deeper.

Finally, his body betrayed him. An involuntary spasm wracked his chest, his mouth opening in a silent gasp. Water rushed in, shocking him back to reality. With a mixture of desperation and defeat, Dexter angled himself upward, his legs kicking furiously as he clawed his way back to the surface.

47

Reluctantly, Dexter surfaced, gasping for air. The car was sinking faster than he could swim. He took several deep breaths, trying to oxygenate his blood as much as possible before diving again.

This time, he angled his body downward, using his arms to pull himself deeper. The pressure increased, squeezing his chest, making each movement a struggle. His eyes strained in the murky depths, searching desperately for any sign of the Corsa.

There! A dark shape loomed before him, barely visible in the gloom. The car was sinking fast, air bubbles streaming from the open windows. Dexter's lungs screamed for air as he made a final push towards the vehicle.

He reached the driver's side door first, tugging at the handle. It wouldn't budge. Panic started to set in as he realised the doors were locked. He moved to the open window, peering inside.

Lucy floated limply in her seat, her eyes closed, hair drifting around her face like seaweed. The seatbelt held her in place as water filled the cabin. Dexter reached in, his fingers, numb with cold, fumbling at the seatbelt catch.

It refused to budge. Black spots danced at the edges of his vision, his body desperate for oxygen. With a last, frantic effort, he managed to hit the release. The belt retracted, and Lucy began to drift free.

As Dexter grabbed her arm, Lucy's eyes flew open. In her panic, she began to thrash, fighting against his grip. In the struggle, she inhaled water, bubbles escaping from her mouth as she choked.

Dexter wrapped his arms around her, pinning her arms to her sides. He kicked hard, propelling them both towards the surface. The journey up seemed endless. His muscles screamed in protest, his chest burning with the need to breathe. Lucy was dead weight in his arms, dragging him down.

At the shore, Caroline sat on her haunches, her forearms clamped to the side of her head as she pleaded desperately for Dexter to resurface. She didn't care if it was without or without Lucy Palmer. All she needed was to see her colleague – her friend – poke his stupid, grinning little head above the surface of the water again.

She looked at her phone. How long had he been down there? She didn't know. Too long, surely. She had no doubt Dexter was a stronger swimmer than her. A fitter person, without a doubt. She stood no chance. All she could do was wait. Wait and hope.

48

Just as he thought he couldn't hold on any longer, they broke the surface. Dexter gasped, drawing in great lungfuls of air. He towed Lucy's now-limp form towards the shore, where Caroline was wading out to meet them, water sloshing around her knees.

Together, they dragged Lucy onto dry land, her waterlogged clothes making her feel twice as heavy. Caroline immediately dropped to her knees beside Lucy's motionless body, checking for any signs of life.

'No pulse,' she said, her voice tight with urgency. 'Starting compressions.'

Caroline interlaced her fingers and began chest compressions, counting under her breath. Dexter, still gasping for breath, tilted Lucy's head back to clear her airway, his hands shaking from cold and exhaustion.

'Come on, Lucy,' Caroline muttered, her arms aching

as she continued the rhythmic pressure on Lucy's chest. 'Don't do this. Not now.'

Dexter watched Lucy's face, willing her to show some sign of life. Her skin was pale, almost blue, her lips tinged with an unnatural purple. Water trickled from the corner of her mouth with each compression.

'Rescue breaths,' Caroline ordered, pausing her compressions.

Dexter pinched Lucy's nose and sealed his mouth over hers, blowing two quick breaths. He watched her chest rise and fall, then Caroline resumed compressions.

Seconds ticked by, feeling like hours. In the distance, sirens wailed, backup finally arriving. But for Dexter and Caroline, the world had narrowed to this moment, this desperate fight to bring Lucy back from the brink.

'How long?' Dexter asked, his voice hoarse.

Caroline shook her head, not breaking her rhythm. 'Too long,' she grunted, sweat beading on her forehead despite the chill air.

They continued the cycle – compressions, breaths, compressions. Lucy remained unresponsive. Dexter could feel hope slipping away with each passing moment.

'Come on, Lucy,' he found himself whispering. 'You don't get to check out like this. Not after everything.'

Just as despair began to set in, as Caroline's arms began to tremble with fatigue, Lucy's body convulsed. Water spewed from her mouth as she coughed violently, her eyes flying open in panic. She gasped, a ragged, desperate sound that was the most beautiful thing Dexter had ever heard.

'It's okay,' Caroline soothed, quickly helping Lucy onto her side. 'You're safe now. Just breathe. That's it, nice and easy.'

Lucy continued to cough and gasp, expelling water from her lungs. Her body shook with the effort, each breath a battle. Dexter sat back on his heels, exhaustion washing over him as the adrenaline began to ebb.

He met Caroline's eyes over Lucy's trembling form, a silent understanding passing between them.

49

The gentle hum of the office was absent as a sombre silence filled the room. Elijah leaned back in his chair, a self-satisfied smirk playing at the corners of his mouth. He revelled in the absence of Dexter, savouring the extra space, both physical and metaphorical, that he now occupied in the team.

The door swung open.

Dexter strode in, his face set in grim determination. A collective intake of breath destroyed the stillness. Eyes darted between Dexter and Elijah, anticipating the inevitable confrontation.

Elijah's smirk faltered, replaced by a flash of naked panic. It lasted only a moment before he schooled his features into a mask of indignation. 'What the hell are you doing here?' he demanded, rising to his feet. 'You're suspended!'

Dexter said nothing, moving to stand beside Caroline's desk. She remained seated, her expression unreadable.

Aidan couldn't contain his glee, a wide grin splitting his face as he watched the scene unfold. Sara, however, looked bewildered, her gaze bouncing between Dexter and Elijah as if watching a tennis match.

'I asked you a question, Antoine,' Elijah snarled, his composure slipping. 'What. Are. You. Doing. Here?'

Caroline finally spoke, her voice calm and measured. 'Sit down, Elijah.'

'Like hell I will,' he spat. 'Not until someone explains what's going on.'

The door opened again. Two stern-faced officers in plain clothes entered, their expressions leaving no doubt as to their purpose. One stepped forward. His presence seemed to suck the air out of the room.

'Detective Sergeant Elijah Drummond?' he asked, though it wasn't really a question.

Elijah's face drained of colour. 'Yes?' he replied, his voice suddenly small.

'I'm Detective Chief Inspector Rawlings from the Professional Standards Department. This is Detective Sergeant Patel.' He gestured to his colleague, a woman with sharp eyes and an air of quiet authority.

A ripple of shock ran through the office. Elijah's eyes darted around, searching for an ally, finding none.

DCI Rawlings continued, his tone brooking no argument. 'Elijah Drummond, I am arresting you on suspicion of perverting the course of justice, wasting police time, making false allegations, and misconduct in public office. You do not have to say anything, but it may harm your defence if you do not mention when questioned something which you later rely on in court. Anything you do say may be given in evidence.'

As the words sank in, Elijah's bravado crumbled. His shoulders sagged, and for a moment, he looked utterly lost. 'This... this is ridiculous,' he stammered, but there was no conviction in his voice.

DS Patel stepped forward, producing a pair of handcuffs. 'Please turn around and place your hands behind your back, sir.'

Elijah's eyes widened, the reality of the situation finally hitting him. 'No, wait,' he protested weakly. 'There's been a mistake. Caroline, tell them!'

Caroline met his gaze coolly. 'I'm sorry, Elijah. This is out of my hands.'

The click of the cuffs echoed in the silent office. Elijah's colleagues watched in stunned disbelief as the man who had swaggered among them for so long was reduced to this pitiful figure.

As the PSD officers began to lead Elijah towards the door, he found his voice again. 'This is a mistake!' he cried, looking wildly around the room. 'You can't do this! I haven't done anything wrong!'

Just before he was led out, Elijah's eyes locked with Dexter's. In that moment, all pretence fell away. The fear, the desperation, the knowledge that his carefully constructed world was crumbling – it was all there, naked in his eyes.

Then he was gone, the door closing behind him with a soft click that seemed to echo with finality.

For a long moment, no one moved. The silence was deafening, broken only by the distant sound of Elijah's protests fading down the corridor. Then, as if a spell had been broken, the office erupted into a flurry of whispers and exclamations.

Aidan was the first to approach Dexter, clapping him on the shoulder with undisguised joy. 'Welcome back, mate,' he grinned. 'God, it's good to see that smug bastard get what's coming to him.'

Sara hung back, her face a mask of confusion and disbelief. She opened her mouth as if to speak, then closed it again, her gaze darting between Dexter and the door where Elijah had just been led out.

Dexter offered her a small, tired smile. 'It's alright, Sara. You weren't to know. None of us did, not really.'

Caroline stood, calling for quiet. As the chatter died down, she addressed the team. 'I know you all have questions,' she said, her voice firm but understanding. 'They'll be answered in due course. For now, let's get back to work. We still have cases to solve, and we can't let this disrupt our investigations.'

As the detectives reluctantly returned to their desks, the air thick with unasked questions and stunned disbelief, Caroline turned to Dexter. 'My office,' she said quietly.

Dexter followed her, aware of the eyes on his back. As

he closed the door behind him, he felt a weight lift from his shoulders. It wasn't over – there would be statements to make, evidence to review, a trial to face. But for now, in this moment, he allowed himself to feel the first stirrings of relief.

He was back where he belonged. And Elijah? Elijah was finally facing the consequences of his actions.

'Welcome back, Dex,' Caroline said, a rare smile softening her features. 'We've got a lot to catch up on.'

Dexter nodded, settling into the chair across from her desk. 'It's good to be back, boss,' he said, feeling for the first time in weeks that things might just turn out alright.

Outside, the office buzzed with activity, the team throwing themselves into their work with renewed vigour. There was a sense of a page being turned, a new chapter beginning.

Justice, it seemed, had a way of finding its mark after all.

50

The harsh fluorescent lights of Derek Arnold's office seemed to amplify the tension in the room. Caroline stood before his desk, her posture rigid, while Dexter leaned against the wall, his arms folded across his chest. The air was thick with unspoken words and barely contained emotions.

Arnold pinched the bridge of his nose, exhaling slowly. 'Let me get this straight,' he began, his voice deceptively calm. 'You deliberately called in a suspended officer to assist you on an active investigation?'

Caroline met his gaze steadily, her heart racing despite her outward composure. 'Yes, sir. I did.'

'And how, exactly, am I supposed to explain that to my superiors?' Arnold's voice rose slightly, his frustration evident. He leaned forward, his hands splayed on the desk. 'Do you have any idea of the position you've put me in?'

Caroline fought the urge to look away. She'd known

this moment was coming, had dreaded it even as she'd made the decision to involve Dexter. The familiar internal struggle between following protocol and trusting her instincts gnawed at her.

'Sir, with all due respect,' Caroline began, choosing her words carefully, 'Dexter was innocent. It was obvious he'd be reinstated eventually. If I hadn't called him in—'

'A killer might have overpowered you and escaped?' Arnold finished, his tone skeptical. 'Except you didn't *know* Palmer was a killer at that point, did you?'

Caroline's shoulders sagged slightly. 'No, sir. I didn't. Not for certain.'

Dexter shifted against the wall, about to speak, but a sharp look from Caroline silenced him. His jaw clenched, a mix of relief at his reinstatement and anger at the situation warring within him.

'But I was right, sir,' Caroline continued, her voice firm despite the doubt gnawing at her. 'Lucy Palmer did turn out to be our killer. And going single-crewed would have been disastrous.'

Arnold leaned back in his chair, his brow furrowed. 'You couldn't possibly have known that at the time, though.'

'No, sir,' Caroline conceded. 'But I trusted my instincts. And those instincts led us to solve two murders and prevent a suicide.'

The room fell silent as Arnold considered her words. His eyes flicked to Dexter, who remained silent but watchful, his posture tense.

Arnold sighed heavily, running a hand through his thinning hair. 'Do you two have any idea of the pressure I'm under?' he asked, his voice low. 'We're the smallest force in the country. Every decision, every case, is scrutinised. I'm constantly fighting to maintain our autonomy, to keep major crimes investigations here instead of handing them over to EMSOU.'

He fixed Caroline with a stern look. 'And every time you pull a stunt like this, you make that job harder. You make it harder for me to defend our department, to justify our handling of these cases.'

Caroline felt the weight of his words, the familiar guilt settling in her stomach. But beneath it, there was a flicker of defiance. 'I understand, sir. But with all due respect, our solve rate speaks for itself. We get results.'

Arnold's lips thinned. 'Results aren't everything, you know. Procedure matters. Protocol matters.' He pinched the bridge of his nose, exhaling slowly. 'And there's one thing I still don't understand, Hills. How did we miss the connection between Lucy Palmer and Kevin Hartley for so long?'

Caroline felt a twinge of embarrassment. 'It turns out there was a typo in Hartley's postcode on the PNC. Hartley was apprehended at work and brought straight here. We spoke to Lucy at the house where the party had been held, and it was only when we visited her at home following Sophie Trent's death that the connection was made. A simple clerical error, but it meant the addresses didn't flag up as being the same.'

Arnold's eyebrows shot up. 'A typo? Christ, the things that can slip through the cracks.'

'I know,' Caroline nodded, her voice tight. 'I'm not exactly happy about it myself.'

Arnold's gaze turned to Dexter. 'DS Antoine. I suppose I should address your situation as well.' He paused, seeming to gather his thoughts. 'Your suspension is officially lifted. You're back on active duty, effective immediately.'

Dexter nodded, a small, bitter smile tugging at the corners of his mouth. 'Thank you, sir.'

Arnold's attention returned to Caroline. 'As for you, DI Hills… I hope you realise the position you've put me in. I've got to figure out how to smooth this over with the higher-ups. Again.'

'I understand, sir,' Caroline said, her voice contrite but her posture unyielding.

Arnold waved a hand dismissively. 'Go on, both of you. Piss off out of my office before I change my mind.'

As Caroline and Dexter filed out, Arnold called after them, 'And for God's sake, try to stay out of trouble for at least a week, will you?'

The door closed behind them, leaving Arnold alone with his thoughts and the monumental task of explaining this mess to his superiors. He reached for his phone, already dreading the conversation to come.

Out in the corridor, Caroline and Dexter exchanged a look—relief, triumph, and a touch of apprehension for what lay ahead. The tension between them was palpable, unspoken words hanging in the air.

'Pub?' Caroline suggested, sensing they both needed to decompress.

Dexter hesitated for a moment, then nodded. 'Yeah. I think we need to talk.'

51

Karen stood at the kitchen window, her fingers curled tightly around a mug of tea that had long since gone cold. The late evening sun cast long shadows across the well-manicured garden, a stark contrast to the turmoil raging within her.

Lucy. The name reverberated through her mind, bringing with it a tidal wave of emotions—love, guilt, horror, betrayal. How had it come to this? Her niece, her daughter, a murderer.

The sound of a car pulling into the driveway jolted Karen from her reverie. Kevin. Her stomach clenched. He would want answers, answers she wasn't sure she could give without destroying what little remained of their family.

She watched as Kevin got out of the car, his movements slow and heavy, as if carrying the weight of the world on his shoulders. In a way, she supposed he was.

Their world had shattered the moment Lucy had been arrested, and the pieces were still falling.

Karen's gaze drifted to the framed photos on the mantelpiece. Lucy's gap-toothed grin at six, arm slung around a pigtailed Emily. The girls at their school prom, faces alight with promise and hope. Emily.

The name sent a jolt through Karen's body, a mixture of desire and gut-wrenching guilt. She closed her eyes, memories washing over her unbidden.

Emily at five, all skinned knees and infectious laughter, following Lucy around like a devoted puppy. Emily at fifteen, whispering secrets with Lucy at sleepovers, their giggles drifting down the hallway. Emily at twenty, a woman now, her eyes meeting Karen's across the dinner table with a heat that made Karen's breath catch.

'Stop it,' Karen whispered to herself, pressing her palms against her eyes as if she could physically push the memories away. But they kept coming, relentless.

The first time Emily had kissed her, tentative and questioning, in the shadows of the garden during Lucy's twenty-first birthday party. The way Emily's touch had ignited something in Karen she thought long dormant. The thrill of stolen moments, the weight of guilt that grew heavier with each encounter.

The sound of Kevin's key in the lock snapped Karen back to the present. She took a shaky breath, steeling herself. He deserved to know the truth. About Lucy, about Emily, about all of it. But could she bring herself to deliver the final blow to their already fractured family?

'Karen?' Kevin's voice, tired and strained, called from the hallway.

She cleared her throat. 'In here,' she managed, her voice sounding foreign to her own ears.

Kevin appeared in the doorway, his face etched with lines of worry and fatigue. 'Any news?' he asked, the hope in his voice barely concealing the fear beneath.

Karen shook her head, unable to meet his eyes. 'Nothing new,' she said softly. It wasn't technically a lie. There was no new information, just the terrible truth she'd been carrying since the police had called yesterday.

Kevin sighed, collapsing into a chair at the kitchen table. 'I just don't understand,' he murmured, more to himself than to Karen. 'Our Lucy, arrested. There must be some mistake.'

Karen's hand tightened around her mug. *Oh, Kevin*, she thought. If only it were a mistake. If only their sweet, clever Lucy hadn't committed such horrific acts. If only Karen's own actions hadn't set this terrible chain of events in motion.

She found herself moving towards him, drawn by the pain in his voice. She placed a hand on his shoulder, feeling him lean into her touch. The simple gesture of trust made her heart ache. How could she tell him? How could she not?

'Kev,' she began, her voice barely above a whisper. 'There's something—'

But Kevin cut her off, reaching up to squeeze her hand. 'We'll get through this, love,' he said, his voice thick with emotion. 'Whatever's happened, whatever Lucy's done or hasn't done, we'll face it together. As a family.'

Karen felt tears prick at her eyes. Family. The word felt like a knife twisting in her gut. They had taken Lucy in, given her a home, a family, when she had lost everything. And how had Karen repaid that trust? By betraying them all with Emily.

Emily. Lucy's best friend since childhood. The daughter Karen had never had. The woman who had awakened desires Karen had long thought buried. The affair had been exhilarating, intoxicating, and utterly, unforgivably wrong.

And now Emily was dead. Murdered by Lucy. The thought made Karen's knees weak. She gripped the back of Kevin's chair, steadying herself.

'Karen?' Kevin's voice was laced with concern. 'Are you alright?'

She nodded mutely, not trusting herself to speak. How could she tell him? That their daughter had killed two people? That one of those people had been her lover? That she, Karen, was indirectly responsible for this nightmare?

'I'm just tired,' she managed finally. 'It's been... a lot.'

Kevin nodded, understanding in his eyes. Understanding that made Karen's guilt flare anew. 'Why don't you go lie down for a bit?' he suggested gently. 'I'll make us some dinner.'

Karen nodded, grateful for the reprieve, however brief. She needed time to think, to decide. As she made her way upstairs, her gaze fell on Lucy's bedroom door, closed now as if to shut away the memories of the happy, loving girl who once lived there.

In her own bedroom, Karen sank onto the bed, her body heavy with the weight of secrets and regret. Her eyes landed on a framed photo on the bedside table—Lucy and Emily at the beach last summer, arms around each other, faces split with carefree grins.

Karen picked up the frame with trembling hands. How had it all gone so wrong? She traced Emily's face with a finger, remembering the softness of her skin, the warmth of her smile. Then Lucy, her sweet, complicated Lucy. The niece she had promised her sister she would protect. The daughter she had sworn to love and nurture.

She had failed them both so completely.

Karen clutched the photo to her chest, years of memories crashing over her. Lucy's first day of school, Emily holding her hand as they walked through the gates. Teenage sleepovers filled with whispered confidences and stifled giggles. Family dinners where Emily was as much a fixture as any of them. And later, stolen glances across rooms, the electric thrill of forbidden touches, the intoxicating taste of Emily's lips.

A sob escaped Karen's throat, the sound raw and painful in the quiet room. She had to tell Kevin. He deserved to know the truth, all of it. About Lucy's crimes, about her affair with Emily. About how her actions had set in motion a tragedy that had destroyed so many lives.

But as she sat there, the weight of her guilt pressing

down on her, Karen found she couldn't move. Couldn't breathe. Couldn't face the thought of seeing the love in Kevin's eyes turn to disgust and betrayal.

And as the evening drew to a close, Karen sat motionless on the bed, trapped between the past she couldn't change and the future she didn't know how to face.

52

The Wheatsheaf pub hummed with the usual evening chatter, a welcome backdrop to the tumultuous thoughts swirling in Caroline's mind. She and Dexter had managed to snag a quiet corner table, away from the bustling bar and regular drinkers. The warm glow of the overhead lights cast a soft sheen on their pints as they sat in companionable silence, each lost in their own reflections on the events of the past few weeks.

Caroline watched Dexter over the rim of her glass, noting the slight furrow in his brow, the tension in his shoulders. He'd been through hell, and she couldn't help but feel partly responsible. She opened her mouth to speak, but Dexter beat her to it.

'I've been thinking,' he began, his voice low and serious. 'Maybe it's time for a change.'

Caroline's eyebrows rose, a knot forming in her stomach. 'What kind of change?'

He shrugged, his fingers tracing patterns in the condensation on his glass. 'I'm thinking of resigning. Or maybe transferring to another force.'

'Dexter,' Caroline said, leaning forward, her voice tinged with disbelief. 'You can't be serious. After everything we've been through?'

'That's just it, though,' he replied, meeting her gaze with a mixture of weariness and resolve. 'After everything we've been through. The suspension, the doubt, the experience down at the water... it takes its toll. Makes a man wonder if it's all worth it.'

Caroline nodded, understanding all too well the weight of their profession. 'I know it's been rough. God, do I know. But you're back now. Vindicated. We need you here, Dex. The team needs you.'

Dexter's lips quirked in a half-smile, a hint of his usual sardonic humour peeking through. 'Do you? Or do you just need someone to keep you out of trouble?'

'Both,' Caroline admitted with a wry grin. 'Probably more the latter, if I'm honest.' Her expression sobered. 'Look, I'm not going to tell you what to do. It's your life, your career. But please, just... think about it, alright? Don't make any hasty decisions. Give it some time.'

Dexter studied her for a moment, then raised his glass in a mock toast. 'I'll think about it. That's all I can promise for now.'

Caroline nodded, accepting that it was the best she could hope for at the moment. She was about to press further when the pub door swung open, admitting Aidan and Sara.

Aidan's face split into a wide grin as he spotted them, practically bouncing over to the table. His enthusiasm was a stark contrast to the serious conversation that had preceded his arrival.

'There they are!' he exclaimed, pulling up a chair. 'The dream team, back in action. God, it's good to see you two together again.'

Sara followed more sedately, offering a small smile as she sat down. Caroline noticed a hint of tension around her eyes, a slight stiffness to her movements.

'Oh, I almost forgot,' Caroline said to Dexter. 'Sara put a referral in for the waste dumping to be investigated by a specialist environmental crime team. They've taken it on. With great interest, I hear…'

'I should imagine so, too,' Dexter replied. 'Great work, Sara.'

Aidan was practically vibrating with excitement, either oblivious to or choosing to ignore the undercurrent of tension. 'I still can't believe we nailed Elijah. What a piece of work, eh? To think he had us all fooled for so long.'

At the mention of Elijah, Dexter's demeanour shifted. A spark of pride ignited in his eyes, his posture straightening. 'I knew it,' he said, his voice carrying a hint of triumph. 'I told you lot from the start there was something off about him. If only you'd listened to me sooner.'

'You certainly did,' Aidan agreed, raising his glass. 'To Dexter's impeccable judgement! And to justice served!'

Dexter grinned, clinking his glass against Aidan's. The weight that had been pressing on him seemed to lift, if only momentarily. 'Vindicated and victorious!'

Caroline noticed Sara stiffen, her face paling slightly. She opened her mouth to intervene, to change the subject, but Dexter, caught up in the moment, ploughed on.

'I mean, did you see the look on his face when they took him in? Classic guilty conscience. I bet he thought he'd got away with it, the smug bastard. All that charm, that fake concern... and in the end, it was all just a front for a cold-blooded bastard.'

Sara abruptly stood up, knocking her chair over. The sound cut through the general hubbub of the pub, drawing a few curious glances. 'Excuse me,' she muttered, her voice tight. Without meeting anyone's eyes, she quickly made her way to the exit.

Aidan's smile faltered as he watched her go. He glanced at Caroline and Dexter, a mixture of guilt and concern on his face. 'I should...' he gestured towards the door, already half-rising from his seat.

Caroline nodded, understanding passing between them. 'Go on. Make sure she's alright.'

As Aidan hurried after Sara, Caroline turned to Dexter, who looked utterly bewildered by the sudden turn of events.

'What just happened?' he asked, confusion evident in his voice. 'Did I say something?'

Caroline sighed, taking a long sip of her drink. She'd hoped to avoid this conversation, at least for tonight, but it seemed there was no putting it off now. 'I think we need to have a chat about Sara and Elijah,' she said, preparing to fill Dexter in on the complexities he'd missed during his suspension.

Dexter's brow furrowed, a mix of concern and curiosity replacing his earlier triumphant expression. 'Sara and Elijah? What about them?'

As Caroline began to explain, she couldn't help but wonder how this new dynamic would affect their team going forward. The celebration had taken an unexpected turn, leaving an air of unease hanging over their table. It was a stark reminder that in their line of work, things were rarely simple, and victory often came at a price.

53

The cool night air hit Sara like a slap as she burst out of the Wheatsheaf, her chest tight with a maelstrom of emotions she couldn't begin to name. She stumbled a few steps, bracing herself against the rough brick wall of the pub. The cheerful sounds from inside seemed to mock her, a stark contrast to the confusion and anger roiling within.

Sara closed her eyes, trying to steady her breathing. This was all wrong. A mistake. It had to be. Any moment now, someone would come out and tell her it had all been a misunderstanding. Elijah would be released, and everything would go back to normal.

'Sara!' Aidan's voice cut through the fog of her thoughts. She heard his footsteps approaching but couldn't bring herself to look at him.

'Sara, wait,' he called again, closer now. His voice was laced with concern, but also something else. Pity? The thought made her bristle.

She pushed off from the wall, turning to face him with a forced calm she didn't feel. 'I'm fine, Aidan. I just needed some air.'

Aidan stood a few feet away, his brow furrowed with worry. 'Are you sure? After what happened in there...'

'What happened in there,' Sara said, her voice tight, 'was a lot of premature celebration over a massive error in judgment.'

Aidan's expression shifted, a mix of surprise and something that looked frustratingly like sympathy. 'Sara, I know this must be difficult to hear, but—'

'No,' Sara cut him off, her calm facade cracking. 'You don't know. None of you do. Elijah is innocent. This is all just a terrible mistake.'

Aidan took a step closer, his voice gentle. 'Sara, I understand you care about him, but the evidence—'

'To hell with your evidence!' Sara snapped, her composure shattering completely. 'Do you have any idea how easy it is to plant evidence? To misinterpret facts?'

Aidan flinched at her outburst but held his ground. 'Sara, please. I know this is hard, but we have to face the facts. His phone records, the DNA...'

Sara shook her head violently, feeling tears beginning to well up. She blinked them back furiously. 'No. You're wrong. You're all wrong about him. Elijah wouldn't... he couldn't...'

She turned away from Aidan, unable to bear the look of pity in his eyes. 'You don't know him like I do. He's kind, he's compassionate. He helps people, for God's sake!'

Aidan sighed, running a hand through his hair. 'Sara, I know you want to believe in him. But sometimes people aren't who we think they are.'

Sara whirled back to face him, anger flashing in her eyes. 'And sometimes the police make mistakes. You're all so eager to close this case, you're not even considering other possibilities!'

'We've considered every possibility,' Aidan said, his own frustration beginning to show. 'We've followed every lead, checked every alibi. The evidence all points to Elijah staging his own attack and framing Dexter.'

'That's ridiculous!' Sara exclaimed. 'Why would Elijah do something like that? He has no motive!'

Aidan's expression softened. 'Sara, I know this is hard to hear, but think about it. Has Elijah ever done anything that made you suspicious? Anything that didn't quite add up?'

Sara opened her mouth to deny it, but suddenly memories began to surface. The late-night phone calls he'd step out to take. The times he'd been vague about his whereabouts. The way he'd sometimes look at her with an expression she couldn't quite read...

'No,' she whispered, more to herself than to Aidan. 'No, it doesn't mean anything. Everyone has secrets. It doesn't make him... it doesn't mean he'd do something like this.'

Aidan's voice was gentle when he spoke again. 'Sara, I'm so sorry. I know how much he means to you. But we have to face the truth, no matter how painful it is. The evidence is overwhelming.'

Sara felt her legs give way beneath her, and she sank to the ground, her back against the pub wall. Aidan crouched beside her, close but not touching.

'He was supposed to be different,' she said, her voice barely audible. 'After everything... my family, all the disappointments... He made me feel like I mattered. Like I was worth something.'

Aidan's hand hovered near her shoulder, as if he wanted to comfort her but wasn't sure if his touch would be welcome. 'You do matter, Sara. With or without Elijah. You've always mattered.'

She looked up at him then, really looked at him for the first time that night. The concern in his eyes, the gentle set of his mouth – it was all so different from Elijah's carefully cultivated charm.

'How can you say that?' she asked, her voice cracking. 'After everything that's happened, how can anything matter?'

Aidan's expression softened further. 'Sara, I've known you for years. I've seen your dedication to the job, your compassion for victims, your determination to find the truth. Those things haven't changed. They still matter. You still matter.'

Something in his tone made Sara's heart skip a beat. She searched his face, looking for any sign of insincerity, but found none.

'Aidan,' she began, not quite sure what she wanted to say.

But before she could continue, the pub door swung open, spilling light and noise into the quiet night. Caroline's voice called out, 'Aidan? Sara? Are you out here?'

The moment shattered. Sara scrambled to her feet, suddenly aware of how close Aidan was, how vulnerable she'd allowed herself to be.

'I should go,' she said quickly, wrapping her arms around herself. 'I need some time to... to think about all this.'

Aidan stood as well, concern etched on his features. 'Are you sure? I can call you a taxi if you'd like.'

Sara shook her head. 'No, I'd rather walk. Clear my head a bit.'

'Alright,' Aidan said, his reluctance clear. 'But promise me you'll text when you get home? Just so I know you're safe.'

A ghost of a smile flickered across Sara's face. 'I will. And Aidan... thank you. For coming after me, for... everything.'

As Sara turned to leave, Aidan called after her, 'Sara?'

She paused, looking back at him.

'Whatever happens,' he said softly, 'you're not alone in this. Remember that.'

Sara nodded, unable to speak past the lump in her throat. She turned and walked away, her mind a whirlwind of conflicting thoughts and emotions.

Aidan watched her go, his heart heavy. He wanted to follow her, to make sure she was okay, but he knew she needed space. Time to come to terms with the harsh reality of Elijah's betrayal.

He remained rooted to the spot, the memory of Sara's vulnerability, the almost-moment they'd shared, playing on repeat in his mind. The urge to protect her, to somehow make this all better, warred with his professional detachment and his own complicated feelings.

'Aidan?' Caroline's voice came again, closer this time. 'Is everything alright?'

He turned to see her approaching, concern etched on her face.

'Not really,' he admitted. 'But it will be. Eventually.'

Caroline nodded, understanding passing between them. 'Come on,' she said gently. 'Let's go back inside. I think we could both use a drink.'

As they headed back into the pub, Aidan cast one last glance in the direction Sara had gone. Whatever happened next, he knew one thing for certain: nothing would be the same after tonight. For Sara, for himself, for their entire team. The road ahead would be difficult, but as he stepped back into the warmth of the Wheatsheaf, Aidan made a silent promise to himself and to Sara.

He would be there, whatever she needed, however long it took. Because some things, some people, were worth fighting for.

54

The harsh fluorescent lights of the prison visiting room cast an unflattering pallor over Sara's face as she sat, hands clasped tightly in her lap. The room buzzed with muted conversations, but Sara barely registered them. Her heart raced, a steady drumbeat of anticipation and nerves.

A buzzer sounded, and Sara's head snapped up. There he was.

Elijah.

He looked different in his prison uniform, the vivid orange a stark contrast to his usual sharp suits. His hair was longer, slightly unkempt, but his eyes—those eyes that had once made Sara's knees weak—still held that magnetic intensity.

'Sara,' he breathed, a smile spreading across his face as he sat down opposite her. 'God, it's good to see you, babe.'

Sara returned the smile. 'Hello, Elijah.'

'I wasn't sure you'd come,' he said, leaning forward.

His voice was low, intimate. 'But I knew... I knew you'd understand. That you'd see through all this nonsense.'

'I... I had to see you,' Sara said. 'To hear your side of things.'

Elijah's eyes lit up, a predator scenting prey. 'Of course, of course. I knew you'd want the truth. Not that rubbish they're all spouting.'

He reached across the table, his fingers brushing Sara's. She leaned into his touch.

'It's all a misunderstanding, babe,' Elijah continued, his voice earnest. 'A witch hunt. They're jealous, you see. Of my success, of our relationship. They couldn't stand to see us happy.'

Sara nodded, her eyes wide and trusting. 'I thought it might be something like that. It just... it didn't make sense. The Elijah I know would never do those things.'

Elijah's smile widened, triumph glinting in his eyes. 'Exactly. You know me. Better than anyone. You know what we have is real.'

He squeezed her hand, and Sara allowed a small, tremulous smile to cross her face. 'I've missed you,' she whispered.

'I've missed you too, babe,' Elijah replied, his voice thick with emotion—or what passed for emotion with him. 'But we'll get through this. You and me, yeah? Once I'm out of here, we'll start fresh. Maybe leave Rutland behind, start somewhere new. How does that sound?'

Sara bit her lip, as if considering. 'It sounds... nice,' she said softly. 'But how... how did this all happen? I mean, the evidence they have...'

Elijah's face darkened momentarily before smoothing out into a reassuring smile. 'It's all circumstantial. Nothing concrete. My lawyer's working on it. We'll have it sorted in no time.'

He leaned in closer, his voice dropping to a whisper. 'I need you, babe. Your support, your love. It's what's keeping me going in here. Knowing that you believe in me, that you're waiting for me. You are waiting for me, aren't you?'

Sara met his gaze, allowing a single tear to slip down her cheek. 'Oh, Elijah,' she breathed.

Elijah's smile grew triumphant. He thought he had her. Hook, line, and sinker.

Sara took a deep breath. This was it. The moment she'd been waiting for, preparing for. She straightened in her chair, squaring her shoulders.

'No,' she said, her voice clear and strong. 'I'm not waiting for you.'

Elijah blinked, confusion clouding his features. 'What?'

'I'm not waiting for you,' Sara repeated. 'I'm not supporting you. And I certainly don't believe in you.'

The change in Elijah's demeanour was instantaneous. The charm fell away, replaced by a cold, hard anger. 'What are you playing at?'

Sara laughed, the sound devoid of humour. 'Playing? Oh, that's rich coming from you. I'm not the one who's been playing games. That's been you, all along.'

'Babe, you're confused,' Elijah said, reaching for her hand again. 'Let me explain—'

Sara jerked her hand away. 'Don't touch me,' she snapped. 'And don't call me "babe". I'm not confused, Elijah. For the first time in a long time, I'm seeing things clearly.'

Elijah's jaw clenched. 'You don't mean that. You're upset, I understand. But babe, what we have—'

'What we had,' Sara interrupted, 'was a lie. Every touch, every whispered promise, every secret shared. It was all part of your game, wasn't it? Your endless need to manipulate, to control.'

'That's not true,' Elijah protested, but his eyes darted away, unable to meet Sara's steady gaze.

'Isn't it?' Sara leaned forward. 'You know, I've spent so long turning it all over in my mind. Every moment, every conversation. Trying to figure out where it all went wrong. But I realised something, Elijah. It was wrong from the very beginning.'

Elijah's face hardened. 'You don't know what you're talking about.'

'Don't I?' Sara's voice was quiet but firm. 'I think I do. I think I finally understand you, Elijah. The real you. Not the charming facade you put on, but the cold, calculating man underneath. The man who would do anything, hurt anyone, to get what he wants.'

She saw the flicker of panic in Elijah's eyes, quickly masked by anger. 'You're making a mistake,' he growled. 'After everything I've done for you-'

'Everything you've done for me?' Sara's laugh was bitter. 'You mean isolating me from my friends? Making me doubt myself? Using me as your alibi while you framed an innocent man? Yes, Elijah, you've done so much for me.'

Elijah's mask slipped, revealing a glimpse of the fury beneath. 'You ungrateful little—'

'What?' Sara challenged. 'Go on, say it. Show me who you really are, Elijah. Not that I need to see it. I already know.'

She stood, looking down at the man she had once thought she loved. 'You know, I came here thinking I needed answers. An explanation. But I realised something, sitting here, listening to you spin your lies. I don't need anything from you. Not answers, not apologies, not closure. You don't have that power over me anymore.'

Elijah's composure crumbled entirely. 'Sara, please,' he begged, reaching for her. 'You can't leave me. I need you. I love you.'

Sara stepped back, out of his reach. 'No, Elijah. You don't love me. You don't know how to love anyone but yourself.'

She turned to leave, then paused, looking back at him one last time. 'Goodbye, Elijah. I hope you find what you're looking for. But you won't find it with me. Not anymore.'

As Sara walked away, her steps steady and sure, she heard Elijah calling after her. But his voice faded, drowned out by the sound of her own heart, beating strong and free. For the first time in longer than she could remember, Sara felt light. Unburdened.

She stepped out of the prison into the bright sunlight, taking a deep breath of fresh air. Ahead of her, the future stretched out, unknown but full of possibility. Sara smiled, a real, genuine smile that reached her eyes.

Whatever came next, she was ready for it.

WANT MORE?

I hope you enjoyed *No Way Out*.

If you want to be the first to hear about new books — and get a couple of free short stories in the meantime — head to:

adamcroft.net/vip-club

Two free short stories will be sent to you straight away, and you'll be the first to hear about new releases.

For more information, visit my website: **adamcroft.net**

ACKNOWLEDGEMENTS

When I came to write this section, I looked back at what I'd written for the previous Rutland book, *Moment of Truth*. And it's a good job I did, because otherwise I would have written almost exactly the same thing.

Unfortunately, that does make it rather tricky to write this without mentioning it was a particularly difficult book to write, took me far longer than I would have liked, and that I needed to summon immense willpower to sit down and finish it.

But I'm glad I did. As a result, I think (and hope) *No Way Out* is my best book yet. The early readers certainly seemed to think that's the case, so now I'm going to stick my fingers in my ears and go 'la la la'.

Through gritted teeth once again, I owe a huge debt of thanks (and a few more life-size cardboard cut-outs of Richard Osman) to Mark Boutros, who spent more time than he needed to, helping me batter the plot into shape. Although, with a newborn baby in his house, I'm sure he was grateful for the distraction and that *he* actually owes *me* one.

Huge thanks also go to Lucy, Manuela and Karina for

their early insights and read-throughs. Any remaining silly errors are therefore entirely their fault.

To my cover designer, Nick Castle, for designing another fantastic cover.

To Graham Bartlett, former Chief Superintendent and City Commander of Brighton & Hove Police, for all his help and advice on police procedure.

To Jonny Young for his extraordinary local knowledge and willingness to help me find a location to sink a Vauxhall Corsa.

To you, of course, for buying this book and providing that little nudge towards me sitting down and writing the next one. The support you – and other readers – show me is incredible.

While we're talking about incredible people, I've saved the best til last (and I've got to say that, else I won't get fed). My biggest debt of gratitude goes to Sarah, for all the phenomenal love and support she provides in so many ways. Unfortunately for her, she was the first person to read *No Way Out* in its original state, and was invaluable in helping me craft it into its final form. Not only that, but she's the most wonderful partner, mum and step-mum in the world, and I'll fight anyone who says otherwise.

A SPECIAL THANK YOU TO MY MEMBERS

Thank you to everyone who's a member of my VIP Premium readers club. Active supporters get a number of benefits, including the chance of having a character named after them in my books. In this book, PCs Amanda Robinson and Paul Wardle were named after subscribers.

With that, I'd like to give my biggest thanks to my small but growing group of VIP Premium supporters: Richard Allen, Jean Baker, Steve Barratt, Richard Barrett, Carole Beeton, Ruth Boulton, Elizabeth Brown, Kathleen Burley, Eileen Carter, Emma Chen, Susan Clark, Rosemary Cook, Ann Cooper, Sally-Anne Coton, Esther Cross, Shirley Davies, John Davis, Angela Edwards, Gillian Edwards, Barbara Evans, Diane Fletcher, Mary Fortey, Valerie Foster, Wanda Frye, Karina Gallagher, Clare Garner, Nigel Gibbs, Estelle Golding, Teresa Goodbun, James Graham, Angela Green, Glynis Hall, Sheila Hall, Kerry Hammond, Patricia Harris, Cheryl Hill, Irene Hughes, Linda Johnson, Tyler Johnson, Doreen Jones, Jennifer Kelly, Chloe Kim, Beverley Lewis, Christine Martin, Sandra Murphy, Jenny Mustoe, Zoe Nguyen, Megan O'Brien, Joyce Parker, Sophie Patel, Janice Pearson, Dorothy Phillips, Jacqueline Price,

Kathleen Reed, Kerry Richards, Kerry Robb, Janet Roberts, Amanda Robinson, Michael Robinson, Ellen Robson, Olivia Rodriguez, Sylvia Russell, Emma Sanders, Pamela Scott, Nigel Sherlock, Ann Sidey, Karina Sienna, Shane Smith, Elaine Smith, Susan Stone, Maureen Taylor, Robert Thomas, Carol Thompson, Peter Tottman, Bethan Trueman, Brenda Turner, Samuel Walden, David Walker, Paul Wardle, Wendy Watson, Helen Weir, Mary White, Beryl Williams, Kev Wilson, Margaret Wilson, Pauline Wood, James Wright and Marlene Young. You're all absolute superstars.

If you're interested in becoming a member, please head over to **adamcroft.net/membership**. Your support is hugely appreciated.

EXCLUSIVE MEMBERSHIP BENEFITS

Are you an avid reader of my books? If so, you can gain access to exclusive members-only books, content and more.

By subscribing to VIP Premium, you'll get a whole host of benefits and additional perks — and supporting me and my work directly.

Here are just a few of the benefits you can enjoy:

- **Up to 30% off** all online shop orders from adamcroft.net
- **Early access to new books** — up to *2 weeks* before release
- A **free ebook** of your choice
- **Free short stories**, not available anywhere else
- Have a **character named after you** in future books
- Access to **exclusive** videos and behind-the-scenes content
- A **personalised video message** from me
- Unlimited **free UK postage** (and reduced international shipping)

- **Your name in the Acknowledgements** of every new book
- Access to **exclusive** blog posts

To find out more, or to join today, head to **adamcroft. net/membership.**

HAVE YOU LISTENED TO THE RUTLAND AUDIOBOOKS?

The Rutland crime series is now available in audiobook format, narrated by Leicester-born **Andy Nyman** (Peaky Blinders, Unforgotten, Star Wars) and **Mathew Horne** (Gavin & Stacey, The Catherine Tate Show, Horne & Corden).

The series is available from all good audiobook retailers and libraries now, published by W.F. Howes on their QUEST and Clipper imprints.

W.F. Howes are one of the world's largest audiobook publishers and have been based in Leicestershire since their inception.

W.F.HOWES LTD

QUEST

ADAM CROFT

With over two million books sold to date, Adam Croft is one of the most successful independently published authors in the world, having sold books in over 120 different countries.

In February 2017, Amazon's overall Author Rankings briefly placed Adam as the most widely read author in the world at that moment in time, with J.K. Rowling in second place. And he still bangs on about it.

Adam is considered to be one of the world's leading experts on independent publishing and has been featured on BBC television, *BBC Radio 4*, *BBC Radio 5 Live*, the *BBC World Service*, *The Guardian*, *The Huffington Post*, *The Bookseller* and a number of other news and media outlets.

In March 2018, Adam was conferred as an Honorary Doctor of Arts, the highest academic qualification in the UK, by the University of Bedfordshire in recognition of his services to literature.

Adam presents the regular crime fiction podcast *Partners in Crime* with fellow bestselling author and television actor Robert Daws.